FREE WILLY 2

That night Jesse dreamt that he heard the faint cry of orcas coming through the deep fog. They just kept calling and calling . . .

He opened his eyes. It was early. The light filtered through the tent and the air was damp and cold. There, he heard it again, so faint it might have been a bird or even his imagination. But Jesse didn't think so. An orca was out there somewhere, crying for help.

Todd Strasser has written many award-winning novels for young and teenage readers. Many of his books are based on films, including *Free Willy*, *The Pagemaster* and *Richie Rich*.

FREE WILLY 2

By Todd Strasser
Based on the screenplay written by
Karen Janszen and Corey Blechman
and John Mattson
Based on characters created by
Keith A. Walker

PUFFIN BOOKS

To Sarah, David and Flora Samis

PUFFIN BOOKS

Published by the Penguin Group
Penguin Books Ltd, 27 Wrights Lane, London W8 5TZ, England
Penguin Books USA Inc., 375 Hudson Street, New York, New York 10014, USA
Penguin Books Australia Ltd, Ringwood, Victoria, Australia
Penguin Books Canada Ltd, 10 Alcorn Avenue, Toronto, Ontario, Canada M4V 3B2
Penguin Books (NZ) Ltd, 182–190 Wairau Road, Auckland 10, New Zealand

Penguin Books Ltd, Registered Offices: Harmondsworth, Middlesex, England

First published in the USA by Scholastic Inc. 1995
First published in Great Britain in Puffin Books 1995
1 3 5 7 9 10 8 6 4 2

Puffin Film and TV tie-in edition first published 1995

Typeset by Datix International Ltd, Bungay, Suffolk
Printed in England by Clays Ltd, St Ives plc
Set in 12/14 pt Monophoto Palatino

1

The sky over the ocean was blue and dotted with cottony white clouds. The sun's rays shimmered on the cold clear waters below. Waves creased the ocean's surface. Beneath the waves, thick shafts of sunlight tunnelled down into the dark depths. A high-pitched jabber of squeals and whistle-like calls pierced this liquid world. They told all who listened that a family of orcas was coming.

The mother, Catspaw, led the way. She was the largest, the strongest and the most serious. Behind her followed her children, spouting, chattering, playing in the waves. First came Luna, so called because of the white crescent-shaped patch on her dorsal fin. She always stayed close to her mother's tail. And following them came a medium-sized male, his dorsal fin curled sideways and with three black spots on his throat.

His name was Willy.

More than two years had passed since Jesse had helped him escape from the adventure park aquarium. Now those years of captivity were just a distant memory. Like his fellow killer whales, he knew no boundaries. The vast Pacific Ocean was his home.

He had just one problem . . . Littlespot, the youngest member of the family, named because of the small dark spot under his chin. Nothing was more annoying than a kid brother who wouldn't leave you alone. No matter where Willy went, Littlespot followed. If Willy leapt out of the water, Littlespot was right behind him. If Willy spy-hopped, there was Littlespot, poking his head out of the water beside him.

The only way Willy could shake Littlespot was to dive into the dark cold depths, where the younger orca was afraid to follow. So Willy dived . . . down, down, down to where the deep blue waters finally blotted out the sun and the pressure was so strong it hurt his ears.

Somewhere between Willy and the surface, Littlespot lingered in the water, puzzled, unhappy, and afraid to go any deeper. Suddenly, everything went dark! Littlespot froze in fear. Looking up, he saw a huge, dark shape churning through the waters above. It was enormous! Gigantic! Seized with terror, Littlespot squealed for help and raced blindly away.

Deep below, Willy heard both the churning propellers and his little brother's cry. Unlike Littlespot, Willy had seen these huge ships before and he knew they wouldn't harm him. But Littlespot didn't know that. Instantly feeling protective and forgetting how annoying his little brother could be, Willy raced upwards.

He found Littlespot careering around in frantic circles of fear. Willy swam up to him and nudged him with his nose. Feeling his big brother near by, Littlespot quickly calmed down. Together they swam out from under the shadow of the ship and rejoined Catspaw and Luna.

Soon the orcas were again frolicking in the waves, while the huge oil-tanker was just a dot on the horizon, steaming steadily towards Seattle. Neither the whales nor those on board the ship could possibly suspect that some day their paths would cross again, with tragic results.

Jesse sat behind the controls of Glen's boat, the *Little Dipper*. Jesse was fourteen now, taller, stronger, less wary of the world around him. His hair was still blond and shaggy, but now a few blond whiskers had started to thicken above his upper lip. He still lived with Glen and Annie Greenwood. This was probably the best thing that had ever happened to him. It was hard to believe that, before they'd taken him in, he'd lived on the streets and stolen food in order to survive. Life was a lot better, now that he didn't have to worry about where his next meal was coming from.

The *Little Dipper* was an old wooden boat that Glen had painstakingly restored. It had a white hull and a wooden centre console for steering.

'What's this?' Jesse asked Glen, who was standing behind him in the boat, explaining how everything worked.

'The throttle,' Glen said. 'It has three positions. Push it ahead and you go forward. In the middle you're in neutral. Pull it back and you go in reverse.'

Out of the corner of his eye Jesse saw something

in the distance. He grabbed a pair of binoculars off the console and pressed them to his eyes to have a closer look.

'Come on, Jesse,' Glen said. 'Pay attention.'

But Jesse had other things on his mind. He quickly put down the binoculars, gripped the side of the boat and vaulted over.

'Jesse!' Glen gasped.

But it was too late. Jesse had gone overboard . . .

. . . And landed in the Greenwoods' driveway. The boat was on a trailer, hitched to the back of Glen's car.

Jesse walked slowly down to the end of the driveway, careful not to appear to be in a rush. He pulled his harmonica out of his pocket and played a few riffs. The person he'd seen in the binoculars was riding up the street on her bike. Her name was Andrea Smith, and she was a pretty girl with long brown hair and braces on her teeth.

'Hi, Jesse.' Andrea stopped her bike in the street and smiled when she saw him.

'Hey, what's up?' Jesse stopped playing the harmonica and smiled back. In the past year his whole attitude towards girls had changed. Previously, they'd basically been human beings who looked and smelled slightly different and who could make up the numbers in a baseball team when you couldn't find enough boys. Recently, however, they'd become something completely different. Now Jesse found girls attractive, alluring and deeply puzzling.

'You coming to the beach tonight?' Andrea asked. 'There's gonna be a big bonfire.'

'Can't,' Jesse said, playing it cool. 'I have to pack for vacation. We're going up to San Juan Island.'

Andrea looked disappointed. 'Too bad. See you when you get back.'

'Yeah.'

Andrea started to ride away. Jesse smiled and waved. He was disappointed, too, but he knew better than to show it. Besides, Andrea would still be around when he got back after the holiday.

Jesse turned around and headed back up the driveway. Suddenly he noticed a car parked at the kerb. He recognized it immediately. It belonged to Dwight, the social worker who'd placed Jesse with the Greenwoods.

Jesse felt a slight chill of apprehension, and he quickened his step. It had been a while since Dwight had paid them a visit. Jesse didn't think he was due to come again until around Thanksgiving.

A moment later he pushed through the front door of the house and went into the living-room. Annie and Glen were sitting on the couch. Dwight was sitting in the easy chair.

'Hey, Dwight, how'd you sneak in?' Jesse asked, giving him a high five and studying his face for a clue.

'You were busy,' Dwight replied. He looked pretty glum.

Jesse felt the chill run through him again. He'd

6

had two good years. If the social worker had bad news, he didn't want to hear it.

'Yeah, well, I'm starving,' Jesse said. 'Guess all that boating made me hungry.'

He hoped everyone would laugh, but they didn't. Jesse turned to Dwight. 'Staying for dinner?'

Dwight shook his head.

Now Jesse knew there'd be no avoiding it. 'Hey, what is it?'

'Maybe you should sit down,' Annie said.

It was serious. Jesse felt his chest grow tight. He remained standing and looked at Dwight.

'I have bad news, Jesse,' the social worker said. 'We found your mother in New York City. I'm afraid she's passed away.'

His mother? Found? Dead!

'No.' His chest felt so tight that he couldn't breathe. He couldn't believe it. Not his mum!

'I can't tell you how sorry I am,' Dwight said.

'It can't be.' Jesse could feel the blood draining from his face. He couldn't accept this. Not his mother . . .

'Jesse . . .' Annie had tears in her eyes.

Jesse stepped backwards, as if trying to get away from it. He'd always known he'd see his mother again. *He'd known it!* This couldn't be true. They were saying that he'd *never* see her now.

Jesse said the first thing that popped into his head. 'I should have gone to look for her.'

'She didn't want to be found,' Dwight said.

But Dwight didn't know. No one knew. Jesse could feel a huge pain welling up inside him. 'I should have tried to help her.'

'There's nothing you could have done,' Glen said.

'Yes,' Jesse insisted.

'It's not too late to help her, Jesse,' Dwight said.

'What?' Jesse stared at him, not understanding.

'She left somebody behind,' Dwight said.

Jesse didn't get it. 'Like who?'

'You have a brother,' Dwight said. 'Well, he's a half-brother, actually. He's eight years old.'

A brother? The thought shocked Jesse. 'Where?'

'He was living with her. In New York.'

The words ripped through Jesse's heart. How come his mum had kept this brother and not *him*?

'Forget it,' Jesse said angrily. 'I don't want a brother.'

They all looked at him with shocked expressions on their faces. Fury swept through Jesse like a hurricane.

'But, Jesse . . .' Annie started to get up.

'Don't you get it?' Jesse shouted at them. 'I don't want some stupid brother! I want my mother back!'

Annie tried to put her arms round him, but Jesse pulled away from her and headed for the door. *Bang!* He slammed the door behind him and got out of the house. The next thing he knew, he was running, running . . . as if, somehow, if he ran far enough he could get away from it all.

3

He was sitting on the edge of a dock, looking down at the water. He'd run out of running room — and, anyway, there was nowhere left to go. Tears were falling from his eyes, making little splashes in the seawater, a dozen feet below. His mother was gone. She'd always been gone, but now ... she'd never come back. And she'd betrayed him. Everyone had said she couldn't take care of a child. But she had. She'd had this other child.

The wooden planks of the dock creaked behind him. Jesse turned and saw Glen approaching. He wished Glen would leave him alone — but that was what was both good *and* bad about Glen and Annie: they always came after him.

Glen sat down next to him on the dock. For a while neither of them said a word. But Jesse couldn't keep bottled up what he was feeling inside.

'How could she ditch me and then have another kid?' he asked angrily. 'How come she kept him and not me?'

'I don't know,' Glen said.

Jesse felt the anger slowly start to drain out of him. He'd learnt long ago that there was no point in asking questions where his mother was concerned. No one had the answers. A deep sadness washed through him. He felt his shoulders sag with hopelessness. The tears fell faster.

'I really thought I would see her again,' he said with a sniff. 'I thought, if I was really good, I would get her back.'

'Take it from me, Jesse,' Glen reassured him. 'You are really good.'

If there was one person he could talk to, one person who he knew wouldn't make fun of him, it was Glen. Jesse looked up at him and wiped his eyes. 'What do I do? I always thought I'd see her again. Now Dwight says she's gone, but I can't let go of her.'

'You don't have to let go of her,' Glen said. 'She's part of you. She'll always be a part of you.'

Jesse nodded. Until he'd met Glen and Annie, he'd never taken much notice of what grown-ups said. But Glen was always straight with him. Jesse wanted to stop crying now, but the tears wouldn't stop falling. He turned away and stared down at the water.

'It's the cold air,' he said. 'It makes my eyes run.'

'Yeah.' Glen patted him softly on the back. 'I get that, too.'

*

Later, they were walking back towards the house. Jesse's eyes were dry now.

'So, uh, Dwight had some more news,' Glen said. 'Your brother's coming tomorrow. He's going to stay with us for a couple of weeks.'

'Huh?' Jesse gave him a look of disbelief. 'From New York?'

'It's called Kinship Care,' Glen explained. 'It's actually the law, Jesse. You're his only known relative. He's supposed to stay with us until Dwight can place him with a family.'

But Jesse already knew what might happen. 'Or until Annie falls in love with him and never lets him leave.'

Glen rolled his eyes. 'Don't say that.'

Jesse shook his head. He didn't want that kid near him. 'This sucks, Glen.'

'Tell me about it,' Glen said. 'He's related to you, isn't he?'

Jesse stared at him, puzzled for a second. Then he understood. He'd given Glen a really hard time when he'd first moved in: running away, breaking windows . . . stupid things like that. Glen couldn't be looking forward to going through it all again.

Then Jesse thought of something else. 'When's he coming?'

'Tomorrow morning, early,' Glen said. 'Not much time to prepare, huh?'

'What about our vacation?' Jesse asked.

11

'What about it?' Glen asked.

'You want to bring him?' Jesse asked.

'Looks like we're gonna have to,' Glen said. 'Don't worry. You'll get to see Randolph. We'll still do everything we planned. It'll be fun.'

Jesse studied him closely. 'You really believe that?'

'Ask me in three days,' Glen replied with a wink.

4

The next morning Jesse stayed in bed and listened to music. After a while, he heard the doorbell ring and he knew at once that Dwight had arrived. He could hear voices downstairs, but not what they were saying. A little while later, Annie knocked on his door and came in.

'What's he look like?' Jesse asked, still under the covers.

'Different,' Annie said. 'Why don't you come downstairs and see for yourself.'

'Don't feel like it,' Jesse replied with a shrug.

'Why don't you talk to him?' Annie asked. 'Maybe you could learn something.'

Learn something from an eight-year-old? Jesse gave Annie a funny look. 'Like what?'

'He's been living with your mom for the last eight years,' Annie said. 'You tell me.'

She had a point. Jesse got out of bed and started to get dressed. He washed his face and hands and went downstairs. Dwight had already left. Jesse's half-brother was sitting at the kitchen table while

13

Annie and Glen busied themselves in the kitchen. In a way it reminded Jesse of the scene when *he* had first arrived at the Greenwoods'.

Jesse examined the youngster more closely. He had shaggy brown hair and a pierced ear. He had on a vest made from a tartan shirt with the sleeves torn off, baggy jeans and black boots. He was wearing a baseball cap, backwards. Jesse stepped into the kitchen. Without looking as if he cared at all, he said, 'Hi.'

'Whatever,' the kid said with a shrug, and tried to look uninterested.

Jesse couldn't help being a little amused. In a way it was funny that this eight-year-old twerp was trying to out-cool him. But he kept his guard up. It was important to establish who was cooler.

'Jesse, meet Elvis,' Annie said.

'Elvis?' Jesse repeated, with total disbelief in his voice.

The kid ignored that and looked at Glen. 'So, are you guys rich? Dwight said you were rich.'

'Somehow I don't think Dwight would say that,' Annie said.

'I told Dwight I could only stay with people who were loaded,' Elvis informed them. 'So that it wouldn't be too much of an adjustment.'

Annie, Glen and Jesse exchanged looks. Who did this kid think he was kidding?

'Well, Elvis, I guess that's going to be one of life's little disappointments,' Glen said.

Two points, Jesse thought with a smile. But either Elvis didn't get it, or he chose to ignore it. The kitchen grew really quiet. They could all hear the clock ticking.

'Well.' Annie clapped her hands together. 'I guess it's time to pack up for the trip.'

Elvis stood in the driveway and watched while Jesse helped Glen and Annie lug the suitcases and rucksacks out to the car. Jesse could have felt annoyed, but he forgave the kid for not volunteering to help. After all, he was still brand new here.

Finally it was time to get into the car and go. Elvis got in, carrying a green water-pistol with a bright orange barrel.

'What are you gonna do with that?' Jesse asked, sitting next to him.

'Shoot bears,' Elvis said.

Jesse shook his head and stared out of the window while Glen backed the car and boat-trailer out of the driveway. It was hard to believe that this kid and he had come from the same mother. Then Jesse remembered what he had been like at eight. Maybe it wasn't so hard to believe, after all.

Soon they were heading north in the car, towing the *Little Dipper* on its trailer behind them. Jesse read a car magazine; Elvis just stared out through the window. After a while Annie turned around from the front seat and tried to get him to talk.

'So, Elvis,' she said. 'How'd you get the name?'

'My mom,' Elvis replied. His tone said he thought it was a stupid question.

Glen looked at him in the rear-view mirror. 'Hey, that's how I got my name, too.'

'Whatever,' Elvis said. 'I'm going to be a big movie star, just like my dad.'

'Right,' Jesse said. *That* was a good one.

'My dad's Al Pacino,' Elvis said.

Jesse sighed. Did this kid really think they *believed* all that stuff?

Now Elvis turned to Jesse. 'My friends call me Godfather.'

'You have friends?' Jesse asked, just to make sure the kid knew he wasn't fooling anyone.

'Fans,' Elvis corrected him.

'Give me a break,' Jesse groaned. This kid wasn't the way he had been when he was eight – he was a million times worse. In the front seat Annie and Glen shared a look, as if they couldn't believe him either.

The road they were on started to wind its way along the coast. Suddenly Elvis practically climbed over Jesse in order to point out of the window.

'Hey, the ocean!' he cried, momentarily forgetting to be cool.

'So?' Jesse said, pushing him off.

'My mom loved the ocean,' Elvis said.

16

Jesse glanced at him, wondering about that. Was it true?

'She was born at sea, you know,' Elvis said.

'That's interesting,' Annie said, looking over the front seat at him. Jesse was also interested. He'd never known anything about her background.

'On an aircraft-carrier,' Elvis said. 'Nobody's supposed to know that. It's classified.'

A cloud of disappointment settled over Jesse. For a second he had thought that the kid was telling the truth, but it was just another Elvis story. Jesse was really getting tired of them.

'Do you come with remote?' he snapped, wishing he could press a button and turn him off.

Later that day, they drove the car and trailer on to the ferry that would take them over to San Juan Island. Everyone got out of their cars and stood at the ferry's rail, taking in the crystal-blue waters, pine-tree-covered islands, and the snow-capped mountain peaks in the distance. In between the islands, fishing trawlers were moving slowly, with flocks of squawking seagulls hovering over them like mosquitoes.

Jesse and Elvis stood at the rail near the stern of the ferry. Elvis, of course, was working hard at keeping a bored expression on his face. Half the time Jesse thought he was a jerk, but the other half he couldn't help being curious about him; Jesse had carried so many questions about his mother in his head for so long. And Elvis must have some of the answers. Jesse found himself looking at the boy, wanting to get to know him better.

Suddenly Elvis turned and caught him. 'What are you staring at?' he asked.

'What are *you* staring at?' Jesse shot back defensively.

Elvis shrugged. 'A bunch of water.'

'Shows what you know,' Jesse said. 'These are the straits.'

'They don't look straight,' Elvis said.

'Straits are passages of water connecting bigger bodies of water,' Jesse explained. 'These straits run from the Pacific Ocean through the islands.'

Elvis pointed at an island they were passing. A large wooden structure stood near the shore and a group of people were standing on it. 'That an amusement park?'

'No, it's a whale-spotting station.'

'You mean, where they paint spots on whales?' Elvis asked.

Jesse rolled his eyes. This guy acted so clever in some areas and so stupid in others. Just then, a commotion broke out at the ferry's stern. Everyone was pressing towards the rail and pointing at the ferry's wake. Jesse worked his way back and joined them. A pod of black-and-white orcas was surfing and playing in the ship's wake.

Jesse looked carefully, but Willy wasn't among them. He felt a wistful pang inside. More than two years had passed since he'd seen his friend. He often wondered if he'd ever see Willy again.

5

The ferry docked in Friday Harbour, a small seaside town with a boat marina and a main street that was lined with old buildings. The Greenwoods climbed back into their car and drove off the ferry and through town. From there they drove along the coast of San Juan Island until they came to the campsite where they planned to spend their holiday.

The campsite was located on the side of a hill overlooking the Haro Strait, the body of water that ran from the Pacific Ocean, through the islands between the State of Washington and the Island of Vancouver. As Jesse helped the Greenwoods unpack, he spotted the grey concrete rest-rooms with a couple of payphones on their outside wall. Picnic tables and barbeque pits were also spread around the grounds.

They set up two tents, a large blue one for Annie and Glen and a smaller, beige one for Jesse and Elvis. Once again, Elvis sat and watched while the others worked. That annoyed Jesse, but he had other, more important things on his mind. As he helped Glen put up the tents, he kept looking down the dirt road that wound through the campsite.

Finally, a light-coloured pick-up truck bounced up the road. Jesse recognized it immediately.

'Randolph!' he shouted and started to run towards the truck.

Randolph was the former caretaker at the amusement park where Willy had been confined. Randolph had helped Jesse free Willy. He was a Haida Indian and had taught Jesse the story of Natsalane, the Indian brave who, according to ancient legend, had brought orcas into the world. Now Randolph worked at the Orca Institute, an organization that studied and protected the killer whales.

Randolph got out of the pick-up and he and Jesse hugged each other. 'Hey, Jess, look at you! You must've grown six inches.'

'Four and a half,' Jesse said.

'Since breakfast,' Glen added as he came up behind them.

Randolph greeted Glen and Annie warmly. Then he nodded at Elvis. 'Is this the brother I've heard about?'

Jesse's half-brother shook Randolph's hand. 'The name's Elvis. I'm half Apache.'

Jesse saw a smile creep across Randolph's face. 'Pleased to meet you, Elvis. The Apache are the sworn enemy of my people.'

Elvis's eyes opened wide. Jesse couldn't help smiling. Way to go, Randolph!

'Really?' Elvis's voice trembled a little.

'No,' Randolph said with a big grin. Then he turned to Jesse. 'Come on, we're going for a ride.'

'Where?' Jesse asked.

'To do some whale-spotting.' Randolph climbed back into the pick-up and Jesse went round to the passenger side. Elvis was following him, but Jesse had had enough of him for now, so he climbed in and slammed the door, leaving Elvis outside.

Randolph put the truck into gear and they bounced down the bumpy dirt road. As he drove, Randolph sifted through a leather bag on the front seat. Then he pulled out a small, primitively carved wooden orca on a string necklace.

'This is for you,' he said, handing it to Jesse. 'From my village.'

'Wow!' Jesse held the carving up and studied it. Sunlight reflected off the red, black and white whale. Randolph reached across and tapped Jesse on the chest with his fingers.

'My people believe your soul lives here,' he said. 'When you wear the necklace around your neck, the orca is close to your spirit.'

'This is great! Thanks.' Jesse put the necklace on. The carved orca rested on his chest.

'I've missed having you around,' Randolph said

as they drove along. 'I don't know many people who have what you have.'

Jesse wasn't sure what Randolph meant. 'What do I have?'

'Medicine roots. It makes you special.'

There was a time when Jesse would have scoffed at that thought. But that was years ago, before Willy.

They rode along in silence for a while.

'Setting Willy free was the best thing I ever did,' Randolph said.

'Me too. The best.' Jesse nodded and gazed out of the window. Down through the trees he caught glimpses of the blue waters lapping against the island's shores. He missed Willy. 'Have you seen him?'

'Willy?' Randolph shook his head. 'No.'

They turned down a narrow gravel road and passed a painted wooden sign that said ORCA INSTI-TUTE. After Randolph had left the amusement park, he had come to work here at the institute, studying and protecting the killer whales. The institute was housed in a log building that was too large to be called a cabin. On the far side of the building was a long dock. Moored there was a thirty-foot cabin-cruiser called the *Natsalane*, after the Indian warrior from the myth. Randolph parked the truck by the dock.

'Where're we going?' Jesse asked.

'Out on the boat.'

'Cool.' Jesse walked out on the dock and climbed on to the deck of the *Natsalane*. Randolph climbed up to the bridge above the cabin and started the engines.

'Take up the stern line and we'll be off,' he shouted.

'You talkin' to me?' Jesse asked.

'Her.' Randolph pointed towards the stern.

Jesse turned and saw a girl come out on the deck. She was slender and tall. She wore a T-shirt and cut-off jeans, and her long brown hair was tucked up under a baseball cap. Some tall girls whom Jesse knew walked around hunched over, as if embarrassed by their height. But this girl stood tall and proud. She was really pretty. Jesse couldn't help staring at her.

'Ahem.' Randolph cleared his throat.

Jesse looked up at him. 'Aren't you gonna introduce me?'

'No,' Randolph replied. 'I want you up here with me. I might even let you steer.'

Jesse climbed up on to the bridge and joined Randolph. The bright sunlight sparkling on the water made him squint. 'Who is she?'

'My orca-spotter,' Randolph replied shortly. He had a rather gruff tone, as if hinting that he didn't want Jesse to go near her. But Jesse kept looking back as the girl coiled the stern line into a neat circle on the after deck.

24

Suddenly and without warning, Randolph shoved a pair of binoculars into Jesse's hands. Then he pointed out into the strait. 'Here, keep your eyes peeled for whales.'

Jesse scanned the water. However, the binoculars swept around towards the stern of the boat, as if they had a mind of their own, and focused on the girl again. Now he could see her more closely: she had a turned-up nose and high cheekbones . . . She was beautiful.

'Hey.' Randolph nudged him with his elbow and pointed out over the bow. 'The whales are out *there*.'

'She is fly!' Jesse whispered.

'Give me a break,' Randolph grumbled. 'She's my god-daughter.'

'What's that?' Jesse asked.

'That means she's not my daughter, but she's *like* a daughter to me,' Randolph said. 'I look out for her.'

'I'd look out for her, too,' Jesse said with a wink.

Randolph let out a big sigh and shook his head. Then he looked back towards the stern and shouted, 'Nadine!'

Jesse suddenly felt nervous. He held his breath as she climbed up to the bridge. Randolph introduced them.

'Hi,' Jesse said, trying not to sound too eager.

'Hello.' She studied him in a reserved manner.

25

'Would you take the wheel, Nadine?' Randolph said. 'I want to take Jesse below and show him the set-up.'

Nadine took the wheel while Randolph and Jesse went down into the cabin. It was filled with electronic equipment: monitors, sonar-screens, tape-recorders, everything you'd need to study whales. Randolph flicked some switches on a tape-recorder, and the reels began to turn slowly.

'Listen to this,' he said. The high-pitched squeals and whistles of whales started to come through the speakers. 'We've been tracking this pod all the way up the Pacific coast.'

He fiddled with the knobs again and the sounds became clearer. 'Each pod has its own distinct dialect, like an accent. It helps us identify them from a distance.'

Randolph kept adjusting the knobs on the tape-recorder, slowly filtering out the background sounds until a single whale-call remained. Suddenly Jesse felt a shiver and got light-headed for a moment. No, it couldn't be . . . He gave Randolph a questioning look.

'I didn't want to tell you until I knew for sure,' Randolph said. 'But we're pretty sure Willy's pod has been in these waters for a couple of days.'

'We have to find him!' Jesse gasped.

'That's why I brought you here.' Randolph patted him on the shoulder. 'But I have to warn you:

Willy's been living in the wild, in the open sea, for the past two years. There's no telling if he'll remember us.'

'He'll remember me.' Jesse was convinced.

'There's no telling what he'll remember or if he'll even be tame,' Randolph warned him. 'I just don't want you to be disappointed.'

'But we have to try,' Jesse insisted.

Randolph nodded. 'Sure. We've got nothing to lose.'

They rejoined Nadine on the bridge. Randolph took the wheel and Nadine slipped on a pair of headphones. Jesse gave her a curious look.

'They're hydrophones,' she explained. 'To listen for the whales.'

Randolph pointed away to the right, and Jesse saw a number of dolphins playing in the waves.

'White-sided dolphins,' Randolph said. 'The lucky ones.'

'Lucky?' Jesse scowled.

'The unlucky ones are in aquariums all over the country,' Nadine said. 'Their normal lifespan in the wild can reach twenty-five years. But in captivity they won't live past the age of four.'

Just then, Randolph cut the engines. The boat rose under the backwash and began to drift. Nadine flicked a switch so that the hydrophone sounds came out through a speaker on the bridge. Jesse could hear a distant rumbling sound like engines, as well as some squeals and squeaks.

'The rumbling sound means there's a tanker out there somewhere,' Randolph said.

'Any orcas?' Jesse asked.

Randolph listened for a moment, then he shook his head and started up the engines again. 'Not here. Let's try Turner's Point. Maybe they're having lunch.'

While Randolph steered, Jesse and Nadine stood near each other, taking turns with the binoculars. After a while, Jesse put them down and shot a quick look at her. Nadine turned and glanced at him. She had a playful glint in her eye.

'So . . .' Jesse wanted to say something, but he couldn't think what.

'Buttons on ice-cream, see if they stick,' Nadine said.

'Huh?' Jesse didn't get it.

'Sew buttons on ice-cream, see if they stick,' Nadine said again. 'It's an expression. Somebody says, "so," and you say —'

'Buttons on ice-cream, see if they stick.' Jesse grinned. 'That's pretty good.'

Nadine smiled back. 'Yeah.'

The boat lurched, making a sudden turn, and both Jesse and Nadine grabbed the rail to keep their balance. Randolph was pointing. In the distance, Jesse saw two whales breach and spout.

'J-pod,' Randolph said. 'Willy's family is usually with them.'

'Let's get closer!' Jesse said excitedly, pressing

against the rail in order to see. He counted at least half a dozen whales diving and surfacing.

'Can't,' Randolph replied. 'We're required by law to stay a hundred yards away.'

A huge orca surfaced, its massive tail flapping out of the water.

'That's Catspaw,' Randolph said, 'Willy's mother.'

Willy's mother! Jesse felt a rush of excitement.

'Look over there!' Nadine pointed away to the right, where three other orcas were surfacing and diving. One was of medium size, the others were small and young.

'Was that them?' Jesse asked.

'Too far away to tell,' Randolph said. 'One looked about Willy's size. The other two were smaller. Could have been his brother and sister, Littlespot and Luna.'

'He's got a brother and sister?' Jesse asked in amazement.

Randolph smiled. 'Yup.'

Jesse picked up the binoculars again and peered through them. A small orca surfaced once more. 'That one's got a white patch on his fin.'

'*Her* fin,' Randolph corrected him. 'That's Luna, Willy's sister.'

Jesse kept the binoculars pressed against his eyes. If Luna was there . . . suddenly a larger orca broke through the surface. Unlike the others, its dorsal fin curled sideways. That could only mean one thing!

'Willy!' Jesse shouted. 'It's him!'

6

'Here!' Randolph picked up a silver whistle from the console and tossed it to Jesse, who blew it hard, just as he used to at the amusement park when he wanted Willy to perform tricks.

But Willy and the other orcas kept moving. Jesse blew the whistle again.

The whales changed direction and headed towards the open ocean, picking up speed. Jesse blew the whistle once more, but the whales were moving away now.

'Why doesn't he hear me?' Jesse asked.

Randolph slowed the boat.

'What are you doing?' Jesse gasped.

'They're hunting now,' Nadine said. 'We can't keep up with them.'

'It's getting late,' Randolph said as he turned the boat around. 'We have a long way back.'

'But it was *Willy*,' Jesse said, as if that alone was reason enough to follow the whales through the night.

'I know, Jess,' Randolph said with a heavy heart.

'We'll try again tomorrow.'

Jesse felt an acute mixture of joy and disappointment. Joy that he'd seen his old friend, and disappointment that Willy had swum away without recognizing him. Was Randolph right? Had Willy forgotten him? He stood beside Randolph and Nadine as they made their way back towards the Orca Institute.

'Why's Willy's fin still bent?' he asked.

'The cartilage grew that way when he was in captivity,' Nadine said. 'Now it'll never change.'

'At least it makes him easy to recognize,' Randolph added.

'I would have recognized him anyway,' Jesse said.

Nadine went below. Jesse stood with Randolph for a while, then he, too, went below. He found her in the cabin, writing in a notebook.

'So, uh, what are you doing?' he asked, still feeling nervous in her company.

'We keep a log of whale sightings,' Nadine explained without looking up.

'How long have you worked for Randolph?' Jesse asked.

'Since he got here,' Nadine said. 'The last two summers.'

'He said something about being your godfather?'

'Yes,' Nadine replied. 'I've known him ever since

I can remember. His dad and my dad were in the army together.'

She closed the notebook and left the cabin. Jesse followed her up and out to the stern deck. They both stood at the rear of the boat, staring out past its wake, back towards the horizon to the place where they'd last seen Willy. The sun was starting to go down and the water was turning dark. The air felt cooler. Nadine hugged herself.

'I worked with Randolph for a summer,' Jesse said.

'I know,' Nadine replied.

'He told you?'

'Uh-huh.'

Jesse realized that he felt a little jealous. He used to work with Randolph, now Nadine did. It was like he was part of the past or something.

'Did Randolph ever tell you that I have medicine roots?' Jesse asked.

Nadine gave him a funny look. 'Let's see 'em.'

'It's not something you carry on you,' Jesse explained. 'It's something inside you.'

Nadine's eyebrows rose slightly. 'Am I supposed to be impressed?'

'Yeah,' Jesse said. 'I mean . . . Well, are you?'

Nadine just rolled her eyes. Jesse felt a bit stupid. Maybe it was better if he kept quiet.

7

They got back to the Orca Institute, then Randolph drove Jesse back to the campsite. All Jesse could think about was going back out on the boat the next day to look for Willy again. Randolph stopped the pick-up. Jesse saw Glen sitting alone on a log by a campfire.

'Set your alarm clock early, Jess,' Randolph said. 'We'll go out at dawn.'

'I'll be ready,' Jesse said, reaching for the truck door. Then he stopped and looked back. 'You do think he'll remember me, don't you?'

Randolph looked back at him and for a moment he didn't reply. Then he took a deep breath. 'I hope so, Jess.'

Jesse knew Randolph would never promise him something that might not come true. 'Well, it was really great. Thanks.'

Randolph smiled. 'My pleasure, Jess.'

Jesse got out and walked over to the fire.

Glen looked up, the light of the orange flames flickering on his face. 'How'd it go?'

'We found Willy,' Jesse said, sitting down on the log. He gazed at the dancing flames and felt the heat of the fire on his face. 'It was so cool. I mean, I only saw him for a second a million miles away, with binoculars.'

'That's pretty good,' Glen said. 'Considering it's been a long time since you last saw him.'

Jesse pictured Willy in his mind, following Catspaw and frolicking in the waves with Luna and Littlespot. 'It must be great for him.'

'To be with his family, you mean?'

'Yeah.' Jesse just kept staring into the fire. He still wondered why Willy hadn't responded to the whistle. Maybe he'd been too far away to hear.

'You think he misses me?' he asked.

'When you're in someone's heart, you stay there for ever,' Glen said.

Two silhouettes appeared at the edge of the light cast by the campfire, then came closer. As the flames lit them, Jesse saw that it was Annie and Elvis. Wow, he'd been so preoccupied with Willy that he'd almost forgotten about the youngster.

'Time to go to sleep, boys,' Annie said, kneeling down and lighting a paraffin lamp. 'Come on, Jesse, let's get the tent ready.'

They went inside the smaller tent and laid out the foam pads and the two sleeping-bags side by side. As usual, Elvis stood and watched.

'All ready,' Annie said, patting Elvis's sleeping-bag.

Elvis didn't budge. 'I can't sleep on the ground.'

'We're all sleeping on the ground,' Jesse said. 'We're camping.'

Elvis pointed at the sleeping-bags. 'How come you have two foam pads and I only have one?'

'We were all supposed to have two,' Jesse said. 'But no one knew you were coming.'

'I have a bad back,' Elvis said.

Jesse just stared at him. The kid was unreal!

'Jesse, why don't you let Elvis have the extra pad?' Annie asked. 'He *is* our guest, after all.'

Grudgingly, Jesse let Elvis have the extra pad. With a smug look on his face Elvis rolled back his sleeping-bag and stuck the pad underneath. Annie left and they both got into their sleeping-bags. Jesse turned down the lamp until it was dark.

'You don't have a bad back,' he said.

'Do so,' Elvis replied. 'I have spasms. Ever since I went bungee-jumping in the Alps.'

Jesse shook his head in disbelief. This kid was so full of lies, it made him want to scream. He sat up in his sleeping-bag and traced an imaginary line between them down the middle of the tent with his finger.

'See this line?' he asked.

'No,' said Elvis.

'Cross it, and I'll kill you,' Jesse said ominously. He lay back down in the dark and closed his eyes. He just wanted to go to sleep and then get up in the morning and find Willy.

'Glen and Annie told me all about you and Willy,' Elvis said.

'Go to sleep,' Jesse said.

'Same exact thing happened to me, two summers ago,' said Elvis.

'Shut up!' Jesse snapped. The guy was like a gnat buzzing round your head that you couldn't get rid of. A total pain.

In the dark, Jesse heard Elvis's sleeping-bag rustle. 'Is *this* the line you don't want me to cross?'

'You're dead,' Jesse muttered.

'Or is *this* the line?' Elvis taunted him.

That was it. If Jesse had to spend one more second in that tent he would strangle the kid. He threw back the sleeping-bag, pulled on his shoes and stormed out.

Outside, Glen was still sitting by the fire. 'Hey, where're you going?' he asked, surprised.

'Out of here,' Jesse grumbled, and he stamped away into the woods.

He walked down through the trees towards the shore. A jetty stuck out into the moonlit water and he walked out to the end of it, then he sat down with his feet hanging over the edge. Everything was quiet. The moonlight glimmered like a million little ripples on the water's surface. Jesse was glad to be alone.

He pulled his harmonica out of his pocket and played a slow, mournful tune. When he finished, he

36

put it down on his leg and yawned. The harmonica slid off his leg and landed with a *plop!* in the dark water below.

'Great,' Jesse muttered. First Elvis, now his harmonica. He leaned over and looked down into the black water as if somehow he might be able to catch sight of it.

KER-SPLASH! The next thing Jesse knew, a huge wall of water rose up and soaked him right through to the skin.

Plap! The wet harmonica landed in his hand. Jesse wiped the water out of his eyes as quickly as he could, then he looked down. A huge black shape with a white throat was staring back at him.

'Willy!' he cried. He couldn't believe it! Willy was there! Right before his eyes! He must've heard the harmonica!

Willy chattered happily at him, spy-hopping and circling slowly, the way he used to when he wanted Jesse to swim with him.

'Come here, Willy.' Jesse knelt at the edge of the jetty and waved excitedly at him. 'Over here.'

Willy came close and stuck his head out of the water. Jesse stroked his cold, wet skin. He'd forgotten how large orcas grew. Willy was about half as long again as the *Little Dipper.*

'Wow, you've grown,' Jesse said happily. 'I guess you're been eating pretty well out here, huh?'

He gave Willy the 'mouth open' signal, and the

big killer whale instantly opened his mouth, revealing his pointed, ivory-coloured teeth and great pink tongue. Jesse rubbed his tongue — Willy always loved that. Jesse still couldn't believe his friend was back. He *knew* all along that Willy wouldn't forget him!

'I missed you, boy,' Jesse said. Suddenly the things he'd been keeping bottled up inside him began to rise to the surface. Jesse felt his spirits quickly shift from happy to sad as his emotions bubbled up.

'You know I lost my mom,' he said.

As if sensing the change in his friend, Willy let out a little wail of sympathy.

'You have your family again,' Jesse said. 'It must feel great. Without my mom, I feel like I'm nobody. Like I'm all alone.'

As if wanting to cheer Jesse up, Willy drifted back a short distance from the jetty, then he did a little spy-hop twirl.

Jesse couldn't help smiling. 'Hey, you remember your old tricks!' he said.

Willy chattered happily.

'Yeah, yeah.' Jesse grinned. 'You always did know how to cheer me up.'

Then he heard a distant call come across the water; it was an orca call. Jesse peered out into the strait, but he couldn't see anything. He knew, though, who was calling. 'That's your mom, right?'

Willy rolled on to one side and waved at Jesse by flapping his fluke, the flipper that extended from his side. Then he turned and disappeared beneath the surface of the water.

Dripping wet, Jesse stood up on the dock. He was filled with excitement. Willy was here! He'd come back!

Jesse walked quickly along the jetty and back through the woods. Ahead, through the trees, he could see the campfire. Glen and Annie were sitting there, snuggling up together, watching the flames. Jesse couldn't wait to tell them the news.

'Hey, guys!' He stood there in his wet clothes, with a big grin on his face.

Annie looked at him; then she turned to Glen and frowned. 'Oh, yeah, Glen, he *really* looks upset.'

Glen looked puzzled, too. 'Go for a swim, Jesse?'

But Jesse had only one thing to tell them. 'Guess what?'

'What?'

'He really does miss me.'

Glen and Annie looked at each other. Then they looked back at Jesse.

'Who?'

'Willy.'

8

The good news was that he'd found Willy again. The bad news was that now he had to go back into his tent and sleep next to that hopeless liar, Elvis. That night Jesse lay in the tent with the paraffin lamp barely glowing. He was so full of excitement at seeing Willy again that he couldn't sleep.

Elvis was lying still in the sleeping-bag next to him. Soon Jesse's thoughts drifted towards Elvis. He couldn't help it. Willy had found *his* mother. Jesse knew he'd never find his. So this kid was as close as he'd get to her.

Curiosity finally got the better of Jesse; he took the lantern and held it close to Elvis's face, as if searching for something that would tell him all about his brother. In the lamplight the guy looked so young. Maybe Jesse shouldn't blame him for trying to make himself sound so big and important. He was just trying to make a place for himself in a world that didn't seem to have much room for him.

Suddenly Elvis's eyes popped open.

Jesse jerked back.

Elvis grinned. 'Caught you.'

Jesse turned out the lamp and rolled over.

'I never sleep,' Elvis said in the dark behind him.

Jesse clenched his fists. He really wanted to kill that kid.

The next time Jesse opened his eyes, it was light outside. Everything was quiet and the air was damp and chilly, so he knew it must be early morning. Jesse unzipped his sleeping-bag and pulled his clothes inside to warm them up before he put them on. He got dressed inside the sleeping-bag and pulled on his baseball cap, then he left the tent. Mister 'I Never Sleep' was out like a light.

Outside, a mist hung in the air and it was very quiet. No one else on the campsite was out of their tent yet. Jesse stuck his head into Glen and Annie's tent. They were both fast asleep.

'Glen, Annie,' he whispered. 'Wake up.'

'Huh?' Glen slowly opened his eyes. 'Wha . . .?'

'It's morning,' Jesse said. 'C'mon, let's go out on the boat with Randolph.'

'You want to lower your voice?' Glen asked with a yawn. 'You'll wake the bears.'

Now Annie opened her eyes. 'Don't you usually get up at noon?'

'Randolph leaves at dawn,' Jesse said. 'It's dawn.'

'Well, you go ahead, Jesse,' Glen said. He rolled over.

'Hey, Jess?' Annie said, just as Jesse was about to pull his head back out through the tent-flap.

'Yeah?'

'Take Elvis.'

Jesse felt himself go cold. 'No way.'

'Go on,' Annie said.

'Aw, come on,' Jesse begged. 'Do I *have* to?'

'Yes.'

Jesse trudged back to his tent and stuck his head in. 'Hey!' he said in a loud voice. 'Wake up!'

Elvis opened his eyes. 'What?'

'I'm goin' out on the boat,' Jesse said. 'Want to come?'

'OK, yeah.' Elvis crawled out of his sleeping-bag and pulled on his cold clothes. Jesse said nothing; he wasn't about to share his camping tricks with this person.

A few moments later, they were on the path through the woods. Elvis was lagging behind.

'Hurry up,' Jesse called over his shoulder.

'I'm walking as fast as I can,' Elvis said.

'Try running.'

'I can't help it if my legs are shorter than yours,' Elvis said.

Jesse slowed a little. 'If Randolph leaves without us, I'll kill you.'

'I have a black belt in karate,' Elvis said.

'Yeah, well, I have laser death-rays out of my eyes,' Jesse shot back.

'Liar,' Elvis said.

'Look who's talking,' said Jesse.

They got down to the dock where the *Natsalane* was tied up. A man wearing a red tartan shirt was filling her fuel tanks. Jesse climbed on board, followed by Elvis. They were on their way to the cabin when Nadine came out and practically bumped into Jesse.

'Oh. Hi!' Jesse was a little flustered.

Nadine just nodded to him and moved on. Jesse stopped and watched her. Then he realized Elvis was staring at him.

Jesse turned and glared at the kid. 'What?'

'Girls are the enemy,' Elvis said.

'*You're* the enemy,' Jesse said and walked away.

'All girls have cooties from the galaxy Andromeda,' Elvis yelled after him.

Jesse found Randolph, busy in the stern of the boat. He'd pulled open a wooden hatch and was working on something below the deck.

'Hey, Jesse,' he said. 'I'm afraid we've got a problem with the bilge-pump.'

'How big a problem?' Jesse asked, wondering how long he would have to wait until they could leave to look for Willy again.

'Hard to say,' Randolph said. 'Could be a couple of hours; could be a couple of days.'

A cloud of disappointment covered Jesse's face.

'I'm sorry,' Randolph said.

Near the cabin, Nadine was putting her notebook in a small pack.

'Sorry?' Jesse said to Randolph, while watching her.

'That you won't get a chance to see Willy today.'

Randolph didn't know that Jesse had seen Willy the night before, and Jesse didn't have time to tell him about it because it looked as if Nadine was on the point of leaving. Jesse reckoned that if he couldn't see Willy today . . .

'See you later,' Jesse said to Randolph.

'I'll let you know when it's fixed,' Randolph said.

'Great.'

Nadine climbed down from the boat and set off along the dock. Jesse followed, a safe distance behind.

'Hey, where're you going?' a voice above him asked.

Jesse stopped and turned. It was Elvis.

'Go back to camp,' Jesse said. 'Tell Glen and Annie I went out on the boat with Randolph. You couldn't go because you get seasick.'

'But that would be a lie,' Elvis said.

'I'm sure you can handle it,' Jesse said. Then he turned and started to follow Nadine again.

'Where are you going?' Elvis called after him.

'None of your business,' Jesse replied.

9

Elvis set off into the woods towards the campsite. Jesse walked in the opposite direction, following Nadine. For a while she followed a trail parallel to the shore. Then she cut down through the woods and disappeared.

Jesse quickened his step until he came to a clearing. In front of him lay a cove of still water, surrounded on three sides by a rocky shoreline. On the fourth side, the cove opened into the wide blue waters of the straits. A short jetty and a small wooden swimming platform floated in shallow water at one side of the cove, while a much longer jetty stretched out from the other side. A bald eagle circled in the air high above. Between the cliffs and the water was a rocky beach dotted with driftwood, boulders and strands of seaweed.

Nadine was sitting on a grassy knoll above the cove, staring out towards the vast blue straits. She seemed to be craning her neck, peering at something he couldn't see. Jesse moved closer.

Suddenly he saw what it was she was looking at:

a pod of orcas, frolicking in the shallow water, surfacing and diving and playing tag. Jesse stared at them, mesmerized. Wait! Did one of them have a curved dorsal fin? Yes! It was Willy! This was his pod!

Forgetting about Nadine for the moment, Jesse moved forward to get a better look. He left the knoll and scrambled down a short rocky cliff to the shore.

Ooops! He slipped on a smooth rock.

Splash! Jesse fell backwards into a small tidal pool.

Nadine stood up and saw him. She looked a little angry as she came down towards him.

'What do you think you're doing?' she asked.

'Sitting in the ocean,' Jesse said, sitting in the tidal pool.

'You followed me, didn't you?' she said accusingly.

'So?' Jesse shrugged.

Nadine seemed to soften slightly. She held out her hand and Jesse grabbed it. She pulled, helping him to his feet.

Jesse waved his arm around. 'What is this place?'

'My favourite place on earth,' Nadine said, climbing back up the rocks towards the knoll.

Jesse followed her to the knoll and sat down. Nadine didn't sit.

'I came here to be alone,' she said.

'We're alone,' Jesse said, not really catching her drift.

About fifty yards out in the water, one of the whales spy-hopped.

'Hey, look at that,' Jesse said.

One after another, the whales spy-hopped, looking like large black-and-white buoys poking out of the water. Nadine sat down beside Jesse and watched.

'Do they come here a lot?' Jesse asked.

'Yes. This is called Rubbing Beach,' Nadine explained. 'Orcas come from all over to rub themselves on the bottom. Sometimes, if you sit here long enough, one of them will come really close.'

'How close?' Jesse asked.

'One once came about ten feet away,' Nadine said. Jesse smiled. 'You call that close?'

Nadine gave him a look. 'These are wild killer whales. They're not pets, not amusement park rides. They don't like humans.'

Jesse pulled his harmonica out of his pocket and started to play. Nadine looked at him as if he was crazy.

'Are you still trying to impress me?' she asked.

'Yeah.' Jesse kept playing. He *was* going to impress her, all right, but not with his harmonica playing.

Out in the deep water, one of the orcas left the pod and started to swim towards the cove. Jesse got up and scampered over the rocks, then down to the short jetty. Nadine followed.

Finally Jesse knelt down on the edge of the jetty and held his hand out. Willy swam up and Jesse stroked his head.

'Hey, open up for a rubdown,' Jesse said, giving the signal. Out of the corner of his eye he saw Nadine watching them with an amazed look on her face. Willy opened his mouth and Jesse rubbed his big pink tongue.

Suddenly a second, smaller orca poked his head out of the water and opened his mouth.

'Hey, this must be your little brother,' Jesse said. 'Randolph told me about him.' He reached over and tried to rub Littlespot's tongue, but the smaller whale quickly ducked under the water.

'Chicken,' Jesse chuckled.

Jesse leaned towards Willy. 'Hey, help me out here. I want to introduce you to somebody.'

Willy nodded. Jesse turned back and waved to Nadine. 'Come meet Willy.'

On the jetty behind him, Nadine hesitated. 'Uh, I don't know.'

Jesse turned back to Willy. 'Willy, this is Nadine. Nadine, meet Willy. Give her a wave and show her how friendly you are.'

Jesse gave Willy the signal. The orca rolled on to his side, raised his fluke and flapped it against the water.

Nadine laughed. 'OK, I'm impressed.'

Willy swam back to Jesse and caught him by surprise, blowing his baseball cap off his head with his blowhole.

'Hey!' Jesse shouted playfully. 'Not fair!'

He got up, pulled off his shirt and shoes and dived into the cove. The water was chilly, but he quickly got used to it. Willy circled round Jesse, then swam close and rubbed up against him. Jesse waved back to Nadine.

'Come on in, the water's fine!' he shouted.

Nadine stayed on the jetty, looking apprehensive. 'Get a grip, Jesse. That's a killer whale.'

'Naw, he's a friend of mine,' Jesse yelled back. Willy swam under Jesse and rose up. Jesse grabbed his dorsal fin and rode him in a big circle round the cove. Nadine scurried along the rocks, trying to keep up. Her expression said she couldn't believe what she was seeing.

Finally, Willy dropped Jesse off near the shore and headed back out towards the pod. Jesse climbed out of the water, and Nadine brought him his shoes and shirt. They stood together and watched as Willy's pod started to swim away.

'That was amazing,' Nadine said. 'I can't believe he let you do that.'

Jesse turned and looked right into Nadine's eyes. She looked straight back at him. He could feel goose-pimples rising on his skin.

'I think he likes it,' he said.

'I think you're right,' Nadine said with a smile.

They spent the rest of the day together, walking along the shore, watching the otters float on their backs and eat fish, and the seals play. After a while, they found themselves standing on some rocks directly below the campsite. Nadine had the binoculars and was watching something. Jesse sat slightly behind her, looking at how pretty she was. Out of the corner of his eye, he saw a splash on the surface of the water and something flew away.

'You see that?' Nadine asked, still watching through the binoculars.

'Uh huh,' Jesse said, although he hadn't really seen anything.

'That eagle came right down and pulled a fish out of the water,' Nadine said. 'You don't see that every day.'

'Nope,' Jesse said. He still hadn't taken his eyes off her. The sunlight sparkled on the earring of two dolphins that hung from her ear. You didn't see a girl like Nadine every day either.

'Uh oh.' Nadine was looking at something else. Jesse looked up. You didn't need binoculars to see the huge long ship chugging past, belching black smoke from its funnel. It was almost completely flat and must have been the length of a couple of football pitches. Its sides were stained with large brown patches of rust.

'That thing's huge,' Jesse said. 'What is it?'

'Oil-tanker.'

'Kind of ruins the view,' Jesse said.

'Tell me about it,' Nadine said ruefully. 'They always come through here like it's their own private highway.'

Jesse took the binoculars and stared at the tanker through them. 'How come it's so low in the water?'

'That's how they look when they're full of oil,' Nadine said. 'A ship that big can carry thousands of gallons of crude.'

'Crude?' Jesse repeated uncertainly.

'Raw, unprocessed oil,' Nadine explained. 'It's totally toxic to all living things.'

They heard someone beating their way through the woods behind them. It was Glen.

'Hey, Glen.' Jesse waved.

'Hi.' Glen waved back.

'Glen, this is Nadine,' Jesse said. 'She's Randolph's grand-daughter.'

'God-daughter,' Nadine corrected him.

'Nice to meet you.' Glen shook Nadine's hand, then he turned to Jesse and pointed at his wrinkled jeans. 'You go for a swim?'

'With Willy,' Jesse said.

A brief scowl crossed Glen's face. 'Hey, that's great. Now, uh, think I could talk to you for a second?'

'Uh, OK.' Jesse didn't know what it was about,

but Glen wouldn't have interrupted them if it wasn't important. He turned to Nadine. 'Wait here. I'll be back.'

Glen headed into the woods and Jesse walked alongside him.

'So what's up?' Jesse asked.

'Elvis saw you and Nadine this morning, down at the cove,' Glen said.

'Oh yeah? Figures he'd spy on me.'

Glen gave him a super-serious look. 'Listen, I was a lot like you when I was your age. But Annie's worried. She wanted me to talk to you about it. She thinks that kind of behaviour can be dangerous.'

Jesse thought he understood; it was because Willy had been in the wild for two years.

'That's what Nadine thought, too,' he said. 'But I know it's safe. I know exactly what I'm doing.'

'I used to think that, too,' Glen said.

'Hey, come on,' Jesse said. 'I'm practically an expert.'

'I used to think *that*, too,' Glen said with a chuckle. He put his arm round Jesse's shoulder. 'I know you're just going with your feelings. You're a good, smart kid. But it can lead to other things.'

Other things? Jesse didn't have a clue what Glen meant. 'Like what?'

'Well . . .' Glen paused and cleared his throat. 'Like sex.'

Jesse stopped and stared at him. Swimming with Willy could lead to sex? 'Glen, are you feeling OK?'

'I'm fine,' Glen said. 'Why?'

'Because I don't know what you're talking about,' Jesse said.

'I'm talking about you kissing Nadine,' Glen said.

'I never kissed Nadine,' Jesse said.

'You didn't?' Glen looked surprised.

'Who told you that?' Jesse asked.

They gave each other blank looks. Then they both blinked as if they'd realized the answer at the same time.

'I'll give you three guesses,' Glen said. 'And the first two don't count.'

Before Jesse could say anything, Glen turned and headed back towards the campsite. Jesse had a definite feeling he was going to take care of Elvis. He made his way back to Nadine. She was still sitting on the rocks, looking out at the straits through the binoculars.

'What'd he want?' she asked.

'Nothing important,' Jesse said. 'Could I use those for a second?'

'OK.'

Jesse took the glasses and focused them through the trees on the campsite. He watched Glen stop in front of Elvis and say something. Then Elvis went into his tent. Glen zipped it closed behind the boy. Jesse handed the binoculars back to Nadine and grinned. Looked like Elvis had just got himself grounded.

'Was that your brother?' Nadine asked. 'He doesn't look anything like you.'

'We have different dads,' Jesse said. He really didn't want to talk about that little pain, so he pointed back towards the straits. 'Any sign of Willy's pod?'

'Maybe they went back to the rubbing rocks,' Nadine said.

'I wonder why they like it so much,' Jesse said.

'Nobody really knows,' Nadine said. 'But it must feel good to them or they wouldn't do it.'

'Jesse?' Glen called down through the trees. 'Dinner time.'

Jesse turned back to Nadine. 'Guess I gotta go. Want to go back to the rubbing rocks tomorrow?'

'OK,' Nadine said.

'Great.' Jesse started back towards the campsite. 'See you then.'

''Bye.' Nadine waved and started back towards the Orca Institute.

Then Jesse thought of something. 'Hey, wait!'

Nadine stopped. 'What?'

'Bring a bathing suit.'

Nadine looked uncertain. 'You sure?'

'Positive!' Jesse waved and turned towards the campsite. He couldn't wait for tomorrow.

10

The next morning Jesse helped Glen launch the *Little Dipper* into the water. Glen said he was going to keep the boat at the jetty in the cove for the rest of the holiday. He wanted Jesse to go out on it with him, but Jesse said he had other plans. A little later, he met Nadine at the rubbing beach. Together they went out on the jetty. Out in the deep water the whales were surfacing and diving as they rubbed themselves on the rocks.

'You bring a bathing suit?' Jesse asked.

'I'm wearing it,' Nadine said.

'Me too.' Jesse unbuttoned his shirt and pulled off his jeans.

'You sure this is OK?' Nadine asked a little nervously as she pulled off her T-shirt.

'Yeah,' Jesse said. 'They don't eat their friends.'

Jesse dived into the clear Pacific water. Nadine followed. They swam out to the swimming platform. Below, they could see the dark forms of Willy, Luna and Littlespot rubbing themselves against the ocean bottom. Jesse took a deep breath and dived down.

Nadine was close behind him. They swam right into the group of whales, then rose with them to the surface.

Jesse's head popped out of the water. Then Nadine's. Then Luna's, Littlespot's and Willy's.

Luna started to chatter happily at them.

'Willy's sister sure likes to blab,' Nadine said with a laugh.

The whales dived again and the humans dived after them. They played like that for a while. Then Jesse noticed that Littlespot had disappeared. He and Nadine swam to the surface and trod water. Jesse looked around.

'What's wrong?' Nadine asked.

'Littlespot. He's —' Jesse didn't finish the sentence. Over on the rocks, Elvis was shooting at Littlespot with his water pistol. Littlespot was squirting water back with his mouth. Elvis laughed hysterically. Jesse felt a cloud forming.

'That little creep,' he said. 'He follows me everywhere.'

'He looks up to you,' Nadine said.

'No way.'

'He does,' Nadine insisted. 'You want to ask him to join us?'

'No,' Jesse said firmly. Then he eyed Nadine curiously. 'Do you?'

'He *is* your brother.'

'Half-brother,' Jesse said. 'Don't remind me.'

It was obvious that Elvis didn't know they were watching him. He ran along the rocks, laughing and shooting Littlespot with the water gun. Meanwhile Littlespot swam alongside, splashing Elvis with his tail.

'Let's leave him alone,' Jesse said. 'It's the first time I've ever seen him having fun.'

Jesse and Nadine kept diving and swimming with Willy and Luna. At one point, Willy started nudging Nadine with his snout. Nadine grabbed Jesse's hand nervously and held on tight. Jesse hoped she'd never let go.

The next time they came to the surface, another whale voice broke the stillness with a shrill whistle and chatter. Willy and his brother and sister spy-hopped for a moment, then all headed out to sea.

'What was it?' Nadine asked.

'Catspaw,' Jesse said. 'I bet she wants to hunt.'

'Too bad,' Nadine said. 'We were having fun.'

They were treading water. Jesse studied Nadine's face. Her wet hair was all plastered down on her head, but he thought she still looked beautiful.

'It doesn't have to end just because they're gone,' Jesse said.

He and Nadine swam towards a small, crescent-shaped sandy beach beside the cove. Tired from all the swimming and diving, they both stretched out on the sand and lay, soaking up the warm sunshine. After a while, Jesse opened his eyes. He was lying on his back and Nadine was propped up on her elbow beside him, looking at him. She had a strange look on her face.

'Uh, what's up?' Jesse asked uncomfortably.

'I was wrong about you,' Nadine said. She started to move her face closer. She closed her eyes. The next thing Jesse knew, her lips touched his. He closed his eyes. Goose-pimples ran up and down his arms. They were actually kissing. This was . . . amazing.

They stayed like that for a long time: lying in the sun, sometimes kissing, sometimes just gazing into each other's eyes. Jesse felt as if his insides were swelling up with emotion. He'd never felt anything quite like it. He wondered whether Nadine was feeling it, too.

The day passed quickly. They swam together, then walked along the beach, looking at rocks and shells and pieces of driftwood. They held hands and kissed. The whole day had a dreamy, magical quality. Jesse had never spent a day like it before.

Then, too soon, it seemed, it had to end. Dinner time was approaching and Jesse realized he was starving.

'I have to get back,' Nadine said. 'Randolph must be wondering where I am.'

'Yeah, I guess I'd better get back, too,' Jesse said.

They climbed back up on the rocks and pulled

their clothes on over their damp swimming costumes. Nadine took a brush out of her pocket and brushed the sand out of her hair. Then she looked at Jesse.

'Let me do you,' she said.

'Huh?' Jesse didn't follow.

'Your hair.' Nadine stood on her toes and started to brush Jesse's hair. Jesse put his hands on her hips.

'There,' she said, when she had finished. She slipped the brush back into her pocket. Jesse still had his hands on her hips. He was gazing into her eyes.

'Thanks,' he said.

Nadine smiled. 'No sweat.'

Then he kissed her again. Every time his lips touched hers, a magical shiver raced through him.

'See you tomorrow?' Nadine said after they pulled apart.

'Count on it,' Jesse said with a wink.

They went their separate ways, Nadine back to the Orca Institute and Jesse back to the campsite. Glen and Annie were just cooking dinner over the campfire when he arrived. They asked him a couple of questions about how he'd spent his day, but when his answers were vague, they didn't pursue it.

Later, when it grew dark, they went into their tents and got into their sleeping-bags. Once again Jesse lay awake, thinking about Nadine, Willy and, finally, his mother. Meanwhile Mister 'I Never Sleep' was out cold in the sleeping-bag beside him. There was one thing that Jesse still couldn't understand. All those years, when he'd been shuttled from one foster home to the next, and then finally had gone to live on the streets with Perry and the rest of those kids . . . All those years, Elvis had been living with his mother.

There was one question Jesse had to ask. He hated waking Elvis up, but he knew he wouldn't be able to sleep that night until he had the answer. He picked up a torch and shone it in Elvis's eyes.

'Wake up.'

Elvis opened his eyes and squinted into the torch's beam. 'Wha . . .?'

'I have to ask you something,' Jesse said.

'OK.' Elvis shielded his eyes. 'Just don't shine that light in my eyes.'

Jesse aimed the torch upwards. 'Did Mom ever talk about before you were born? Like about when she lived out here?'

Elvis was quiet. Jesse was glad he didn't just come out with one of his wise-guy replies.

'No,' Elvis said.

Jesse could feel the weight of disappointment start to settle on his shoulders. 'Did she ever talk about my dad?'

'No.'

Jesse took a big breath then let it out slowly. 'Did she . . . ever talk about me?'

Elvis was quiet again. Then he shook his head slowly. Jesse felt a pain deep in his heart; he rolled on to his back and stared at the roof of the tent. He didn't want Elvis to see his face. How could she not have talked about him? He was her child!

'She had problems,' Elvis said, as if he knew what Jesse was thinking.

'Like what?' Jesse asked.

'She lied all the time,' Elvis said. 'She said she loved me.'

He sounded as though he didn't believe it.

'Maybe she did,' Jesse said.

'She said she'd never leave,' Elvis said.

Jesse could hear the hurt in his voice. He knew exactly how Elvis felt. He hated to admit it, but he and his little half-brother had a lot in common.

11

That night Jesse dreamt that he heard the faint cry of orcas coming through a deep fog. They were calling for help. He tried to find them, but he couldn't see through the fog. They just kept calling and calling . . .

He opened his eyes. It was early morning. The light was filtering through the tent and the air was damp and cold. There — he heard it again, so faint that it might have been a bird, or even his imagination. But Jesse didn't think so. An orca was out there somewhere, crying for help.

He pulled on his clothes and slipped out of the tent. The air was chilly and he reached back in and grabbed a jacket. He pulled it on and then stood perfectly still.

There it was again. Orcas calling. They sounded scared. Jesse hurried down through the woods towards the water. He wondered what could have happened. Had one of them been hit by a boat in the night? Or got caught in a fisherman's gill-net? He stopped to listen again.

He heard the orcas cry. Then *crackle* ... *snap!* A different sound. Made by someone coming through the woods behind him. Jesse spun around. Elvis was working his way down the path, in and around the trees, pushing branches out of his way. Jesse felt a moment of annoyance, but it quickly passed.

'Come on,' he whispered.

Elvis looked up, surprised to see him. Then he nodded and followed Jesse down the trail. Now he could hear the calls more clearly. They were wails, filled with despair. Jesse quickened his pace.

'Hear that?' he said.

'What is it?' Elvis asked, following behind.

'Orcas.'

'They sound sad.'

'Yeah.' Jesse scurried down towards the cove. By now the red sun was peeping over the mountains across the straits. The rippling water sparkled red.

Jesse suddenly skidded to a stop on the dirt path.

'Elvis, look!' He pointed at the cove, down through the trees. Littlespot was spy-hopping in the middle of the cove, calling out plaintively towards the beach, as if something was there. But the rocks were blocking Jesse's view.

Jesse hurried down the path and paused on the rocks; now he could see the beach. A whale was lying, half-way out of the water. She had a white, crescent-shaped patch on her dorsal fin. Small waves were splashing against her sides.

'It's Luna, Willy's sister,' Jesse yelled back to Elvis. 'She's beached!'

He scrambled over the rocks down to Luna. Out in the water, Littlespot came as close as he could, calling out to her unhappily. As Jesse got closer to Luna, he slowed down. Something was wrong. She was bobbing listlessly in the shallow water. Jesse walked into the water and rubbed her head. Slippery oily goo came off on his hands. Jesse stared at them.

'What is it?' Elvis said.

'Some kind of oil,' Jesse replied. He looked back down at Luna. The oil was all over her head. It was even covering her eyes. Whitish mucus was slowly draining out of her blowhole.

'There must've been an oil spill,' Jesse said. 'This is bad. She's really sick.'

'Why's she facing the beach?' Elvis asked.

'They get confused when they're sick,' Jesse said.

'What should we do?' Elvis asked.

'You gotta go wake Glen,' Jesse said. 'Get him down here as fast as you can. No, wait, have him call Randolph first! We'll all try to get Luna back in the water.'

Elvis started to back away. 'What are you gonna do?'

Jesse rubbed Luna's head. 'I'm gonna stay here with her until help comes.'

Elvis turned and started to run back up the beach.

64

Standing, knee-deep in the cove, Jesse patted Luna on the head.

'You're gonna be OK,' he said softly.

But Luna's eyes were dull and the most she could muster was a low, helpless whine.

'Yeah.' Jesse stroked her sides softly. 'Don't feel like talking. I understand.'

It seemed to take forever for Glen and Annie to come. Meanwhile, the sun rose higher and, way out in the strait, Jesse spotted a long, iridescent patch out on the water, reflecting the sunlight in rainbow colours. It must have been oil — but, if it was, there was a lot of it: it stretched away as far as Jesse could see.

Ker-splash! A sudden splash of water caught Jesse by surprise. It was Willy, using his tail to splash water on his sister. Near him, Littlespot also tried to splash water on his sister, but his splashes weren't nearly as effective. Jesse had to back away so that he didn't get soaked. Somehow Willy knew that he had to keep Luna wet. Today the sun would be their enemy. Luna's black skin would absorb the heat and light of the sun; but, if her skin dried out, Luna would die a slow, painful death.

Finally Glen, Annie and Elvis came running down to the beach. Randolph and Nadine arrived in the truck at the same time.

'Jesse,' Glen said, 'what's this whale doing half-way out of the water?'

'It's Luna, Willy's sister,' Jesse said desperately. 'She's sick. I think she's dying.'

Randolph joined them and nodded grimly.

'What's going on, Randolph?' Glen asked.

'Radio says an oil-tanker ran aground on Lawson Reef last night,' he replied. 'The darn thing's leaking crude oil everywhere. It's a major spill. This stuff is poison to everything that lives in the water. It could devastate every form of wildlife around here for miles.'

'What can we do?' Annie asked.

'First thing is, try to help Luna,' Randolph said. He went back to the truck and took some white gauze and a plastic bag out of a first-aid kit. Then he headed back down towards the beached whale. They all watched as he laid the gauze over her blowhole, collecting some of the whitish mucus. Then he dropped the gauze into the plastic bag and sealed it.

'Nadine!' He waved to her.

'Yes?' Nadine came down towards them. Randolph handed her the bag.

'Run this back to the institute,' he said. 'Tell them it's from me, and it's an emergency. They've probably all heard about the spill by now. They'll know what's going on.'

'They gonna analyse it?' Elvis asked.

'Yes,' Randolph said. 'In the meantime, the rest of us are going to try to get Luna back into the water. Let's go.'

Everyone except Elvis, who was too small to help, waded into the inlet and set to work to get Luna off the rocks and back into the water. As soon as Willy saw what they were doing, he stopped splashing his sister and waited.

'OK, now we don't want to hurt her,' Randolph said. 'Glen and Annie, you each take one of her flukes. Jesse and I will take the tail. Each time a wave comes in, we'll try to slide her out on the run-off.'

Luna was nearly as big as Willy. Working together, however, they managed to slide the whale back into the water. But Luna just lay and bobbed in the shallows. Her breathing was still laboured and her eyes were still glassy. Randolph and Jesse stood waist-deep in the water.

'I'm not sure getting her into the water has helped much,' Glen said. 'She still looks pretty sick.'

'She needs something, Randolph,' Jesse said.

'As soon as we heard about the oil spill we called in Kate Haley,' Randolph said. 'She's our vet from the mainland. I'll try to make sure that Luna's the first patient she sees.'

Now that Luna was floating in the small inlet, Willy began to swim in circles round her. Littlespot followed his older brother. Standing in the water, Jesse realized that his friend was swimming straight towards him.

'Look!' Jesse pointed. 'Willy's got oil on him too.'

'But Willy's bigger and stronger,' Randolph said. 'He may be able to fight it.'

As Willy drew closer, Jesse reached out to pet him proudly. 'Way to go, Willy. You helped save your sis —'

Jesse thought Willy would stop and let him pet him, but the big orca swam right past, ignoring him. Surprised, Jesse turned to Randolph.

'What's the matter with him?'

'His sister is dying,' Randolph replied grimly.

Out in the inlet, Willy circled Luna, as if he were standing guard.

'But we're all on the same side, aren't we?' Jesse asked in a concerned voice.

'It's hard to tell what he's thinking right now,' Randolph replied.

12

The news that three orcas were in the cove began to spread. The coastguards arrived and set up an emergency rescue station for all the creatures that would be affected by the spill. They put up a tent and started a communications centre to organize the rescue effort. Tourists and local newspaper reporters began to show up. Soon the police arrived and used yellow tape to keep people back. Meanwhile, down on the beach, Jesse and the others listened to the news on the truck's radio.

'*The* Dakar, *a forty-year-old Liberian oil-tanker, ran aground on Lawson Reef last night, spilling thousands of gallons of raw crude oil into the water.*'

'If it's forty years old, you know it was a single-hulled piece of rusty tin,' said Nadine, who'd come back from the lab.

'Wait a minute,' Annie said. 'I did a story on oil-tankers once. I thought after 1990 they all had to have double hulls to prevent this kind of accident.'

'All the tankers *built* after 1990 had to have them,' Randolph explained. 'If they were built before

1990, they were exempt from the ruling. A few companies had their older ships retrofitted with a double inner lining, but it was strictly voluntary.'

'So, in a perverse way, by mandating double hulls after 1990 that made the older single-hulled ships more valuable to the oil companies,' Annie guessed.

Randolph nodded. 'You learn quick, Annie.'

'But who's paying for all this?' Glen asked, gesturing at the tents and electronic equipment.

'The oil company that owns the *Dakar*,' Randolph said.

'Then they can't be *that* bad, can they?' Elvis asked.

Randolph and the others just gave him a look. No one answered.

'Look, a plane.' Elvis pointed up into the air and they saw a small seaplane with double floats gliding into the cove for a landing.

'That'll be Kate,' Randolph said.

The plane landed then taxied to the jetty where the *Little Dipper* was tied up. It was on the other side of the cove, where the emergency rescue effort was being set up. Jesse and the others watched as a woman wearing jeans and a red jacket climbed out of the plane and was greeted by a man in a blue coastguard uniform. The woman had shoulder-length brown hair and a short fringe. Together they walked along the jetty and into the tented headquarters of the rescue effort.

'Come on, Jesse,' Randolph said. 'We better go talk to her.'

But Jesse hesitated.

'What's wrong?' Randolph asked.

'They look awful busy.' Jesse nodded towards the tent. Dozens of people were rushing around, studying maps or talking on portable telephones. A lot of the activity was centred round a large map of the straits and islands; it had been mounted on a board in the middle of the tent.

'Hey.' Randolph took him by the arm. 'This is for Willy and his brother and sister.'

They approached the tent. Just as Jesse had feared, the people inside gave them funny looks, as if they didn't belong there. When Randolph tried to go inside, a man stopped him.

'Sorry, folks,' he said, 'but we've got an emergency on our hands.'

Randolph brushed right past him, and Jesse followed. A moment later, Randolph came up behind Kate Haley.

'Kate,' he said.

She turned around. As soon as she saw Randolph, she smiled. 'Randolph!'

'I'm glad you're here,' Randolph said, handing her a clipboard he'd been carrying. Jesse noticed that the other people in the tent were looking at him and Randolph differently now.

'So what've we got?' Dr Haley asked, looking down at the clipboard.

71

'Immature female got into the crude oil. Looks like a pretty severe respiratory infection.'

'How long ago was the culture taken?' Dr Haley asked.

'Three hours.'

Dr Haley looked sombre. 'I heard them struggling to breathe after I got off the plane. We better get to her now, before she gets any worse.'

'Are you a doctor?' Jesse asked.

Dr Haley looked down at him as if she hadn't noticed him before.

'This is Jesse,' Randolph said, putting his hand on Jesse's shoulder. 'He's the one who found them.'

In the midst of the whirlwind of activity around them, Dr Haley focused on Jesse as if there was no one else in the tent. 'So, I finally get to meet you,' she said with a smile. 'Randolph's told me all about you.'

Jesse was surprised to hear that.

'If these whales recover,' Dr Haley said, 'finding them when you did will certainly be the thing that saved their lives.'

'*If* they recover?' Jesse repeated nervously. 'Is there a chance they won't?'

'I'm going to do my best, Jesse,' Dr Haley said.

Jesse had heard that tone a voice a million times in his life. It was the tone adults used when they couldn't make a promise. It meant, *Maybe* . . .

'The Zodiac's ready, Kate,' someone yelled from the entrance to the tent.

'Be right there,' Dr Haley said. She turned back to Jesse. She must have seen the worried look on his face, because she gave him a reassuring smile. 'Hey, don't worry. I'm really good at this.'

Dr Haley turned and headed towards the jetty. Jesse gave Randolph a worried look.

'You remember what happened at the adventure park,' Jesse reminded him. 'Willy doesn't like doctors.'

'She's one of the best,' Randolph said.

'*You* know that,' Jesse said. 'But Willy doesn't.'

'Come on,' Randolph said, making his way back out of the tent. 'Let's go watch.'

They climbed up on the rocks overlooking the cove. Nadine was already there, looking through the binoculars. But she wasn't looking at the whales, instead she was looking out to sea.

'What is it?' Randolph asked.

Instead of answering, Nadine handed him the binoculars. Randolph gazed through them, then lowered the glasses. He looked pale.

'What?' Jesse asked.

'The oil slick is moving this way,' Randolph said. 'If Luna doesn't get better fast, she'll be trapped in the cove.'

'Willy will never leave his sister,' Nadine said. 'And Littlespot does everything Willy does.'

At that instant, Jesse realized what she meant. The three whales would stay in the cove. And it would be covered with oil.

'Then Catspaw will lose her family,' he said. He wanted to hold Nadine's hand, but he couldn't with everyone there.

'How's it going?' someone asked.

They turned and found Glen and Annie climbing up the rocks towards them.

'Don't know yet,' Randolph said.

Out in the cove, Dr Haley and a few others were in the inflatable Zodiac, moving towards Luna. Jesse raised his binoculars.

'Oh, no!' he gasped.

'What's wrong?' Annie asked.

'They're going to inject Luna with a needle bigger than my arm,' Jesse said.

'It's got to be that long to get through the layers of blubber,' Randolph said.

'Try explaining that to Willy,' Jesse said doubtfully.

Not far from Luna, Willy spy-hopped, watching the boat approach. As the Zodiac drew close to Luna, it slowed down. The long, silvery hypodermic needle glinted in the sun.

Suddenly, Willy submerged.

'See, he's getting out of the way,' Annie said.

Jesse had his doubts. A second later, the *Zodiac* rose slightly as if something had lifted it from underneath. In the boat, Dr Haley and the others shouted in surprise and grabbed for the sides to hold on. The Zodiac began to move away from Luna.

'Why are they leaving?' Elvis asked.

'Willy's pushing them,' Jesse said, watching through the binoculars. The boat was moving faster and faster. The people on board were struggling to keep their balance.

'He's trying to protect his sister,' Nadine said.

'Yeah, but that means Luna won't get the medicine she needs,' said Elvis.

'You can't expect Willy to understand that,' Randolph said. 'Especially since he's been in the wild for the last two years.'

'But he remembered me,' Jesse said.

'Yes.' Randolph nodded gravely. 'He remembered *you*. But in every other way this is a whole new ball game.'

13

Now that everyone knew Jesse and Randolph were the friends of Dr Haley, they were allowed to come and go in and out of the command centre as they pleased. Jesse and Nadine got to listen in on the TV interviews as the commander of the coastguard explained to reporters how they were putting a boom in the water round the *Dakar* to try to prevent any more oil escaping. Since oil was lighter than water, it always floated on the surface. A boom was a long tube, filled with air, that was laid out round the oil and stopped it drifting everywhere. He added that, despite their best efforts, the winds and ocean currents could still spoil all their plans.

A little while later, a black limousine arrived at the tent and several men got out. They all seemed to focus on one man in a black suit. He had dark hair and an athletic build. He wore wire-rimmed glasses and was carrying a black briefcase.

'Who is he?' Jesse whispered in Randolph's ear.

'His name's Milner and he's from the oil company,' Randolph whispered back.

'What's he doing here?' Nadine asked, bristling.

'He says he wants to help. He's going to meet with Kate in a second.'

Jesse felt himself grow tense. 'That's rubbish. If he wanted to help, how come he let his company use that crummy old oil-tanker?'

'Because his company was gambling that a tragedy like this wouldn't happen,' Randolph replied.

'They were gambling with the lives of millions of sea creatures,' Nadine said angrily. 'Including Willy and his brother and sister.'

Randolph put his hand on Jesse's shoulder. 'Now calm down. Everybody makes mistakes. Not that I'm any fan of oil companies, but let's at least give the man a chance and hear what he has to say.'

Meanwhile Milner and Dr Haley had started to talk. Randolph, Jesse and Nadine moved closer and listened to what they were saying.

'Wait a minute, Dr Haley,' Milner said. 'I asked you what it would take to save these whales. You gave me a shopping list and I provided everything you asked for. I paid for this camp, I got you the boats and equipment, didn't I?'

Dr Haley nodded. 'Yes, you wrote a cheque.'

'And now you're telling me you can't help that whale because her older brother beat you up?' Milner asked.

'These orcas are very agitated,' Dr Haley tried to

explain. 'They don't trust people. You can understand that, can't you? I mean, given the
circumstances.'

'I just want to save these poor whales and avert a
tragedy,' Milner said.

Jesse was surprised that the man sounded so
sincere, but Dr Haley quickly pointed out why.

'I think you want to avert a public relations
nightmare,' she corrected him.

But Milner didn't get angry or defensive. 'Listen,
doctor, by definition an oil company is a public
relations nightmare. Everyone wants their oil, and
they want it cheap, but nobody wants to clean up
the mess afterwards. That's just part of the business.
The reason I'm here is that I can't sit by and watch
innocent lives lost when we could be doing something about it.'

Jesse was surprised when Randolph stepped forward. 'That's an impressive speech. I wonder if you
mean it.'

Milner took off his glasses and cleaned them with a
handkerchief. He squinted at Randolph. 'What if I do?'

Randolph glanced out of the corner of his eye at
Jesse. 'Then I think I can solve your problem.'

Solving the problem of the whales meant talking to
Glen and Annie. A little while later, Jesse, Randolph,
Dr Haley and Milner showed up at the campsite.
Both Annie and Glen looked surprised.

'Where's the party?' Glen asked.

'Right here at the moment,' Milner said, holding out his hand. 'I'm John Milner from Benbrook Oil, and I need to talk to you about Jesse.'

Glen shook his hand and then they all sat down and discussed the plan Randolph had proposed.

'I'm not going to lie to you, Glen,' Milner said. 'This is an awful situation, and my company is to blame for it. It's very important to me that no harm comes to these whales. And that, according to Randolph, is where Jesse comes in.'

'I don't like it,' Annie said, shaking her head. 'We're talking about killer whales. I won't allow you to put Jesse in danger.'

'But it's Willy,' Jesse said.

'He's been living in the wild for two years,' Annie reminded him. 'No one knows what that means.'

'Jesse's just a kid,' Glen told the others.

'I won't allow him to be put in danger either,' Dr Haley said. 'I assure you it will be all right. But we need him.'

'I could help out,' Elvis said. 'Littlespot likes me. I could –'

Glen raised a finger to his lips and silenced Jesse's half-brother. Elvis narrowed his eyes and looked annoyed.

'The point is, Willy trusts Jesse,' Milner said.

'And he doesn't trust you,' Jesse replied.

'Willy thinks he's protecting Luna,' Dr Haley explained. 'But, by keeping us away from her he's really killing her. Jesse is his only friend. Jesse can help Willy and save Luna.'

'You promise no harm will come to Jesse?' Annie asked.

'I promise,' Dr Haley said.

Glen and Annie looked at each other. Jesse could see that they'd reached an agreement.

'OK, Mr Milner,' Annie said.

'Great.' Milner clapped his hands together and smiled.

'Wait a minute,' Jesse said. Everyone turned and looked at him. 'They agreed, but I'm not sure I have.'

'What do you mean?' Milner looked puzzled.

'I'll convince Willy to let you help Luna,' Jesse said, 'but you have to promise to get Willy, Luna and Littlespot back to their mother.'

Milner was quiet for a moment. Then he said, 'I can't promise that. I'm not God, Jesse. I don't know if the whales will get better. And there are a lot of people to answer to here.'

'But it's your oil that's killing Luna,' Jesse said. 'If Luna dies, everybody's gonna see it on the six o'clock news, and everybody's gonna blame you.'

Milner raised his hands in a helpless gesture. 'I'm doing everything I can.'

'Just promise me you'll at least *try* to get them back to their mother,' Jesse said.

Milner nodded. 'All right. I promise.'

Just then, Elvis got up and marched away into the woods. Annie got up and followed him. For a moment Jesse wondered if something was wrong. Then he looked back at Milner.

'OK,' he said. 'Now there's just one thing I'm gonna need.'

'You name it,' Milner said.

Despite the seriousness of the situation, Jesse couldn't help smiling. 'Chocolate,' he said.

14

Jesse didn't know what was going on between Elvis and Annie, but he didn't have time to find out. Every wasted second was a step closer to death for Luna. They all hurried back down to the emergency command post.

A little while later, Jesse was standing on the jetty, looking out into the cove at Willy. His friend was still circling Luna and Littlespot was following him. On the other side of the jetty, Dr Haley and some crewmen were preparing to go out in the Zodiac again.

Jesse loaded a plastic rubbish bag and some other supplies into a small yellow rubber dinghy beside the jetty. Then he got in and began to row. By now people were watching from all over the place. They were on the beach, up on the rocks, even in boats moored outside the cove.

Jesse rowed out to the swimming platform. Dr Haley and her crew stayed on their boat at the jetty, careful not to attract Willy's attention. Jesse tied the dinghy to the swimming platform and climbed up. Sitting on the edge of the platform with his feet in the water, he started to play the harmonica.

Willy didn't respond. He just kept circling Luna. Jesse played louder. Willy *still* didn't react.

Jesse lowered the harmonica from his lips. Could it be that Willy was ignoring him? That he just didn't care?

No. Jesse looked around at the noisy crowd watching them. They were already loud, and getting louder. That was what was making Willy nervous. Willy had always hated noisy crowds. The big whale leapt out of the water as if to shoo them away, but it only made the crowd *ooh!* and *ahh!* and want more.

Jesse waved towards the jetty at Dr Haley. 'You have to get rid of these people,' he yelled. 'They're upsetting Willy.'

Dr Haley quickly gave some orders and the coastguard began ordering people to move back. They even made the boats outside the cove move away.

Jesse brought the harmonica back to his lips and played again. Willy kept circling Luna. Jesse played louder. Willy veered slightly from his course, as if he couldn't decide which way to go. Jesse realized it must be hard for him to leave his sick sister. But he gradually turned away and swam towards Jesse, as if hoping the boy might have some answer to the terrible fate his sister faced.

'Atta boy, Willy,' Jesse said. 'It's me, your friend.'

He knew he'd caught Willy's eye. The big whale swam towards the swimming platform.

Wait a minute! Suddenly Jesse realized that Willy wasn't stopping.

Thunk! Willy hit the platform with his snout. The platform rocked in the water. It seemed as if he was trying to push it away, just as he'd pushed away the Zodiac that morning.

'Willy, it's me, Jesse,' Jesse yelled.

But Willy just backed away then swam forward again.

Thunk! He rammed the platform again. Jesse lost his balance and had to hold on to prevent himself being knocked over.

Bonk! Something else hit the platform, but barely shook it. Jesse looked down into the water and saw Littlespot, imitating his big brother.

Willy backed away again and prepared to charge the swimming platform once more.

'Stop it, Willy. I'm not going to hurt you,' Jesse said. 'I want to help.'

But Willy just glared at him and emitted a low-pitched whistle that sounded to Jesse like a growl.

'Willy . . .?' Jesse couldn't believe his friend would turn on him like this.

The growl was followed by a groan. But it didn't come from Willy, it came from Luna. Both Jesse and Willy turned to look at the sick whale, floating helplessly in the cove. Then Willy turned back to Jesse. Jesse reached into his rubbish bag and pulled out a large salmon. He held it over the water and gave Willy the signal to open his mouth.

'How about some chocolate, huh?' Jesse said. 'For old time's sake?'

Willy eyed the 'chocolate' but didn't move.

'I know you probably eat live ones now,' Jesse said in a soft voice. 'But this is the best I could do. So what do you say? All I want to do is help Luna and get you all back to your mum.'

Willy moved a little closer but then stopped, as if he still couldn't make up his mind.

'Please, Willy?' Jesse said, barely above a whisper.

Willy moved a little closer and opened his mouth. Jesse looked into it and once again saw those teeth, only now they looked bigger. This was a creature which didn't mind eating a full-grown sealion for dinner, and which had even been known to attack polar bears!

Willy came closer. Jesse realized the whale could have swallowed him whole if it wanted to. He held his breath and shut his eyes. He didn't know what Willy was going to do. He believed that the killer whale was his friend, but you couldn't know for sure. Not after two years in the wild. Not after watching Luna get so sick. Jesse felt something nudge the salmon. Opening his eyes, he saw Willy touching it with his big pink tongue. Jesse laid the fish down on Willy's tongue. Willy swallowed it and chattered. He seemed happy.

A distant cheer came from the crowd watching.

A wave of relief swept through Jesse. He leaned forward and patted his friend on the head. 'Hey, that's the old Willy. I promise you I'm not gonna let you down, pal.'

Willy stayed by the swimming platform and let Jesse rub him on the head. With his free hand, Jesse waved at Dr Haley.

'It's OK,' he yelled.

On the Zodiac, Dr Haley give him the thumbs-up sign. She gave her crew an order, and the boat began to move slowly out into the cove towards Luna.

Almost immediately, Jesse felt a shiver run through Willy. Jesse kept stroking him and talking softly.

'That's Dr Haley,' he said. 'She's going to help Luna.'

The Zodiac came closer. Dr Haley leaned over the side and waved at Willy. 'Hi, Willy,' she said with a nervous smile. 'We already met.'

Jesse watched the boat pull up alongside Luna. He could feel Willy's anxiety. Suddenly he had an idea. 'Look, Willy.'

He slid into the water beside the big whale. The crowd gasped. He and Willy swam closer so that they could watch Dr Haley and Luna.

Dr Haley leant over the side of the Zodiac and stroked Luna's head. 'It's going to be OK, Luna.'

But Jesse could hear the whale was struggling for each breath.

'You don't sound so good,' Dr Haley said softly. Then she turned to Jesse. 'We have to get her to raise her fluke.'

Jesse understood why she'd told him that. He turned to Willy in the water. 'You have to show Luna what to do, Willy. If you do it, she'll do it.'

Jesse gave Willy the sign to raise his fluke. But Willy didn't move. Jesse didn't think it was because Willy didn't want to move. It was just that Willy was probably too upset to want to perform tricks.

Jesse gave him the sign again. 'Come on, Willy. For your sister's sake.'

As if Willy had heard him, he raised his right fluke. Near by, Luna watched. Then, slowly, painstakingly, she raised her fluke.

'Way to go, boy.' Jesse stroked Willy on the head.

'That's good, Luna,' Dr Haley said softly. 'That's really good.'

Jesse watched as Dr Haley gave Luna her injection. Once again Jesse turned to Willy and patted him on the head.

'Nice going, Willy,' he said. 'You just saved your sister's life.'

15

They left Willy and Luna alone after that. Jesse swam back to the swimming platform, got the dinghy and rowed it back to the jetty. Dr Haley followed in the Zodiac. Nadine waited on the jetty with a big beach towel.

'Here, you must be cold,' she said, handing Jesse the towel.

'Thanks.' Jesse took the towel and wrapped it round his shoulders. He was aware that Nadine was watching him closely.

'That was really brave,' she said.

Jesse nodded. 'I . . . I had to do it.'

'I know.'

Their eyes locked. Jesse felt the same emotion he'd felt that day when they'd kissed on the beach. He felt drawn to her as if by a magnet, but they were surrounded by other people. He was too shy to do anything.

The Zodiac docked and Dr Haley climbed out.

'We'd better go see what's going on,' she said, heading towards the communications tent. Jesse and

Nadine walked with her.

Inside the tent, John Milner, the man from the oil company, was on the phone. When he saw Jesse and Dr Haley, he quickly hung up and smiled. Jesse couldn't be sure, but it seemed as if Mr Milner was acting in a slightly guilty fashion about something.

'You hit it out of the park, kid,' he said. 'I'm impressed.'

There was something about Mr Milner that sent out warning signals to Jesse, but he couldn't quite work out what it was.

Randolph joined them and patted Jesse on the shoulder. 'Natsalane would have been proud of you,' he said.

'It was the only way to save Luna's life,' Jesse said.

'All we can do now is wait and see how she responds,' Dr Haley said. 'You did good work, Jesse. It took a lot of guts.'

'I was scared to death.' He blurted the words out before he could stop.

Dr Haley smiled. 'Well, I've got news for you. When you've been doing this as long as I have, you'll be twice as scared.'

One of Dr Haley's assistants came up and took Dr Haley and Randolph aside. He pointed at the map of the straits and spoke in sombre tones. When he had finished, Randolph and Dr Haley turned back to Jesse and Nadine. They both looked considerably less happy than they had before.

'What's wrong?' Jesse asked.

'The oil slick,' Randolph said, pointing at the map. 'The currents are pushing it directly towards the cove. We don't have a lot of time.'

Jesse looked at Dr Haley. 'Can't we do anything?'

'Not yet,' she said. 'First we have to see how Luna reacts to the antibiotics.'

There was nothing to be done but wait. The day passed slowly. Much of the relief effort was turned towards the other animals affected by the oil spill. Hundreds of birds, otters and seals, soaked in black oil and too weak to fight, were brought in to be cleaned and saved. But Jesse heard that, for every creature that was saved, a dozen more would die before help could reach them.

As day turned to dusk and the sun slanted through the trees to the west, Jesse sat on the edge of the jetty with Nadine. Willy was no longer circling Luna. As if sensing that something was being done to help his little sister, he now floated near by, watching and waiting. Luna bobbed quietly in the middle of the cove, as if all her strength and energy was being devoted towards getting well again.

On the jetty, Nadine sat with her knees pulled up tight under her chin and her arms wrapped round her legs. She was staring far out at the waters of the straits. Jesse gave her a curious look. He wondered what she was thinking, but didn't want to ask.

'Their mom is probably going crazy from worrying,' Nadine said, as if she knew Jesse was wondering.

'Catspaw?'

Nadine nodded.

'I wish I could tell her not to worry,' Jesse said. 'Luna's going to get better. I know she will. It's all going to be OK.'

To his surprise, Nadine grimaced and looked quickly away as if he'd said something wrong.

'What is it?' Jesse asked.

Nadine turned back and glared angrily at him. 'It's not *all* going to be OK, Jesse.'

Jesse was surprised to see tears appear in her eyes.

'You have to think positive,' Jesse said. 'Luna's young. She's strong. She can beat it.'

'I'm not talking about Luna,' Nadine said. She waved her arm out at the water and islands. 'I'm talking about all of this. It's all *ruined*. This is just your summer vacation. You can go home. But this is my backyard.'

She was right. He would go home, but she had to stay in a world that would now be covered with a slick, poisonous goo. Nadine sniffed and tried to rub the tears out of her eyes. Jesse wished he had something to give her to help mop up the tears. But he didn't have a handkerchief or any tissues. Then he had an idea and reached up to the pocket of his shirt.

Ripppppp! He tore it off his shirt and handed it to Nadine.

'Here,' he said.

Nadine scowled through her tears at him. 'What?'

'I don't have a Kleenex,' Jesse explained. 'This is the best I can do.'

A small appreciative smile curled on to Nadine's lips. She took the pocket and blew her nose into it. Then she held it out towards him.

'Want your pocket back?'

'Naw, that's OK,' Jesse said with a grin. 'You can keep it.'

The smile faded from Nadine's face. Fresh tears started to gather in the corners of her eyes. Very gently, Jesse reached across and wiped the tears away with his fingertips. Then he slid a little closer and put his arm round her shoulders. Together they stared out at the beautiful sight before them. The sun was setting, giving the distant islands a slightly golden glow. The water was blue and calm. It was a sight that had taken Mother Nature millions of years to create. But it would take man and his oil-tankers only a few days to destroy.

It was dark when Jesse got back to the campsite. From the light glowing inside his tent, he knew that

Elvis was already in his sleeping-bag. Jesse pulled back the flap and was shocked by what he saw. Elvis was lying in his sleeping-bag, holding up the carved wooden orca Randolph had given to Jesse. It looked as if he was studying it.

'Who said you could touch that?' Jesse asked as he ducked down and entered the tent.

'The President of the United States,' Elvis replied. 'He announced it on TV. Where were you?'

Jesse was used to Elvis by now. There was no sense in getting cross. Besides, the kid hadn't hurt it or anything. Jesse pulled off his shoes and trousers. 'I didn't know there were any TVs in this campground.'

'Oh, yeah,' Elvis replied without missing a beat. 'Guy across the way's got a twenty-seven-inch Trinitron.'

Jesse slid into his sleeping-bag. One thing you could say for Elvis: he had a fertile imagination. Meanwhile the youngster was looking at the carving again.

'It's pretty cool, huh?' Jesse said.

'Yeah. What's it for anyway?'

Jesse was surprised. Elvis didn't often ask questions. Most of the time he was too busy pretending he already knew the answers. Jesse rolled over and looked at the kid in the warm glow of the paraffin lamp.

'You really want to know?' he asked.

'Not if it's a long story,' Elvis replied.

'Well, it's not too long,' Jesse said, playing along.

'Oh, OK.'

'There was a young Haida Indian named Natsalane,' Jesse said.

'Haida?' Elvis broke in. 'Is that Randolph's tribe?'

'Right,' said Jesse. 'Anyway, he lived a long time ago, like before there were whales.'

'But there's *always* been whales,' Elvis said.

'Chill a little, OK?' Jesse said. 'This is legend. So one day Natsalane got lost and couldn't find his way home. And he carved the first ever whale out of a log.'

Elvis made a face to show he didn't believe it. 'Come off it. A big wooden fish?'

'You want to hear this story or not?' Jesse asked.

'I bet the big wooden fish comes to life and it's a whale, right?' Elvis guessed.

'That's right,' said Jesse.

'And I bet Natsalane gets back to his family, too,' Elvis added.

The words hung between them in the lamplight. *Back to his family* . . . It was something that would never happen for Jesse and Elvis.

'Yeah,' Jesse said softly. 'That's what happened. Natsalane prayed so hard to get back to his family that the whale came to life. And Natsalane rode on the back of the whale all the way home.'

Jesse waited for a wisecrack from Elvis, but this time none came. The kid was thinking about it. He was probably thinking about that word, too . . . Home.

16

Someone was shaking his shoulder. Jesse opened his eyes. It was morning. Sunlight was filtering through the tent fabric. Jesse turned his head and found Elvis looking down at him.

'Why are you on my side of the tent?' Jesse asked, feeling a little irritable about being woken.

'Oh.' Elvis backed away to his side of the tent.

Jesse studied him. 'You're already dressed?'

'Yeah,' Elvis said eagerly. 'Let's go down to the cove and check on the fish.'

The fish ... Orcas ... Willy and his brother and sister. Jesse sat up and started to pull his clothes on.

'They're not fish,' he said. 'They're mammals.'

'What's a mammal?' Elvis asked.

'I'll tell you when you're older.' Jesse pulled on his shoes. He didn't want to have to take time just then to explain it all. A few moments later, he pushed the tent-flaps apart and crawled out. Elvis followed. Glen and Annie were already up, cooking some food.

'Here, Jesse, have some breakfast.' Annie held up a metal camping plate piled high with eggs and sausages.

'I don't have time,' Jesse said. 'I want to go see how Luna is.'

'Eat it on the way,' Glen said, handing Elvis his own plate of food. 'We'll come with you.'

They started down the trail towards the cove, Jesse and Elvis carrying their plates with them.

'Hey, Annie?' Elvis said through a mouthful of food.

'Don't talk with your mouth full,' Annie said.

'They shouldn't be walking through the woods and eating at the same time either,' said Glen. 'If they trip over, they could choke.'

'I just want to know what a mammal is,' Elvis said.

'What?' Annie frowned.

'Jesse wouldn't tell me,' Elvis explained.

'Oh, I see,' Annie said. 'Well, humans are mammals, and so are whales. They're warm-blooded and they give birth to babies instead of laying eggs. And they feed the babies through their . . .'

Annie seemed to get a little tongue-tied.

'Continue,' Glen said with a smile.

'Uh, they feed their babies through their mammary glands,' Annie said.

'Oh, yeah, I knew that,' Elvis said, putting on the 'know it all' act again. 'So, uh, are girls mammals?'

Jesse had to stifle a laugh. Then he saw Randolph and Nadine coming up the path towards them.

'I was just coming to get you,' Randolph said. He looked grim and in a hurry.

'What is it?' Jesse asked him.

'We've got a problem,' Randolph said.

Before Jesse could ask any more questions, Randolph turned and hurried back down the trail. Jesse and the others followed. When they reached the cove, Jesse saw a group of people huddled round something on the shore. Some of the people were on the beach and some were knee-deep in the water.

It wasn't until he got closer that he saw why they were there. It was Luna! Her nose was up on the rocks and she was half beached again. The people crowding round her were trying to get her back into the water. Jesse started down the beach towards her.

'No, Jesse.' Randolph grabbed his arm. 'Nadine will stay here with Luna. You're coming with me.'

'Where?' Jesse asked.

Randolph pointed to his pick-up truck, parked along the road.

'Luna's not any better,' Randolph said. 'We have to try something different.'

'Like what?' Jesse asked.

'I'll explain as we go,' Randolph replied.

'I'm coming, too,' Elvis said, following them.

'Stay here, Elvis,' Randolph said.

Jesse's half-brother stopped. 'But I can help.'

The only thing Jesse could think of was Luna and how to help her. He wasn't thinking about what Elvis needed.

'Not now,' he said quickly. 'This is between me and Randolph.'

Randolph and Jesse jumped into the pick-up. Randolph shoved it into gear and they set off down the road.

'OK, now what's the plan?' Jesse asked.

Randolph glanced at him out of the corner of his eye. 'There are other medicines besides the ones Dr Haley believes in.'

'Indian medicine?' Jesse guessed.

Randolph nodded. 'All medicine comes from the same place, from our mother the Earth.'

Jesse nodded. Now he knew why Randolph had waited until they were alone. There were plenty of people who would have laughed at Randolph, but Jesse wasn't one of them. Besides, nothing Dr Haley could do would help now. Randolph's medicine might be Luna's last chance.

A little while later, Randolph drove the truck into one of those 'scenic view' spots along the road. He pointed out through the truck's window at the straits.

'One of my spotters said Willy's pod was around the point, just past the Noble Straits,' he said. He picked up a pair of long black binoculars and climbed out of the truck. Jesse joined him where he stood at the side of the road, scanning the blue waters.

'There she is,' Randolph said, pointing.

Jesse squinted. 'I don't see anything.'

'Here.' Randolph handed him the binoculars.

Jesse pressed them to his eyes. All he could see was waves. Wait! Something black and white was sticking out of the water. Jesse focused the binoculars on it. It was an orca.

'Who?' Jesse asked.

'Catspaw,' Randolph said. 'She's looking for her family. She'll look for ever, or until she dies of a broken heart.'

Jesse cupped his hands round his mouth. 'Don't give up!' he shouted. 'We'll get them back to you! I promise! You'll be a family again! It's going to be OK!'

He felt a hand settle on his shoulder. It was Randolph.

'I know you want to help her,' the older man said gently. 'But we have to go.'

They got back into the truck and drove further. Soon the road swung away from the coast and into the woods. Randolph pulled off to the side and stopped.

'What's here?' Jesse asked.

'Hopefully, what we need,' Randolph said, pushing the door open. He got out and pulled an old

wooden basket off the back of the truck. With Jesse
following, he started into the woods, stopping here
and there to pick a flower or a plant and a piece of
bark off a tree. Then he stopped and started to dig
with a flat wooden stick round one particular plant.

'Now what?' Jesse asked.

'This is skookum,' Randolph explained. 'We need
the root.'

'Why use a stick?' Jesse asked. 'Why not a shovel?'

'A flattened stick of alder is what my forefathers
used,' Randolph said as he dug. 'Calling upon ancient
spirits to heal sickness is a gift passed down from
generation to generation. My grandmother taught
me. Now I teach you.'

Once the ground had been broken, Randolph
reached down and carefully pulled up a tangle of
bulbous roots. Just as carefully, he brushed the dirt
off them and held them up for Jesse to see. Then he
put them in the basket and moved on. Soon he
stopped at a tree and peeled back a piece of brown
bark. Jesse was surprised to see that a light green
fungus was growing underneath it.

Randolph took out a zip-lock plastic bag. Then,
still taking great care, he used the alder stick to
scrape the fungus off the bark and into the bag.

'The plants and animals are our brothers in the
world,' Randolph said. 'We are of the same family.
Knowing this is part of what it means to have
medicine roots.'

'I guess it doesn't hurt to have zip-lock bags, too,' Jesse commented.

'Don't be a wise-guy,' Randolph said with a wink.

They walked downhill until they came to a small spring of clear water bubbling out of the ground. There they squatted down and started to wash the roots and plants in the cold water.

'Now what?' Jesse asked.

'We take everything back to the institute and make medicine,' Randolph said, getting to his feet.

They rode in the truck back towards the Orca Institute. They were just about to turn into the driveway when they saw Glen and Annie. Annie was jogging towards them, waving and shouting. Glen was following slowly behind her with a fed-up look on his face.

'Hey, guys, wait up,' Annie called.

Randolph stopped the truck and rolled down the window. 'What's up?'

'Have you seen Elvis?' Annie asked.

'No,' said Jesse. 'Why?'

'He's gone,' said Glen. 'And he took my wallet.'

17

Annie explained what she thought had happened. They'd all been so concerned with the problem of Luna that morning that they'd been short with Elvis and had ignored his offers to help.

'He said he wanted to help and I told him not now,' Glen said.

'And I told him to stand back and stay out of the way,' Annie said. 'I broke a promise.'

'What promise?' Jesse asked.

'I promised he could help,' Annie said. 'I even did a spit-shake on it.'

'That's serious,' Glen said.

Jesse knew that when he said this, it was partly Glen's sarcastic sense of humour, but it was also partly true. To a kid of Elvis's age, a spit-shake was an important thing.

'Should we help try to find him?' Jesse asked.

'Don't bother,' Glen said.

Annie gave him a stern look.

Glen rolled his eyes. 'Don't you ever get tired of this crap?' he asked.

'His feelings are hurt,' Annie said. 'He needs us. He just needs someone to give him a break.'

Glen shook his head. 'Why do *we* have to do it? Why do we have to rehabilitate every troubled kid who comes within a mile of us?'

Jesse raised his hand.

'What?' Glen snapped.

'From what Annie told me, you weren't exactly an angel when you were a kid,' Jesse said.

'Who asked you?' Glen said.

Annie smiled at him.

'OK,' Glen admitted. 'I was trouble. I guess this is my punishment.'

Annie wrapped her arms round Glen. 'Tell me you didn't need someone to love you.'

'That's why I have you,' Glen said.

'And what about Elvis?' Annie asked. 'Who does he have?'

Glen sighed. 'You and me and Jesse.'

'Leave me out of it,' Jesse said.

'Jesse.' Randolph gave him a stern look.

'Hey, only kidding,' Jesse said. 'You want us to help you find him?'

'No, you better keep trying to help Luna,' Glen said. 'We'll look for Elvis. We're on an island, so he couldn't have gone too far. We just wanted you to be aware in case you see him.'

'We'll keep our eyes open,' Randolph said, taking the basket off the back of the pick-up. He turned to

Jesse. 'Now come on, we don't have much time.'

'Catch you later.' Jesse waved to Glen and Annie then followed Randolph into the institute.

Inside, in a modern science lab filled with modern equipment, Randolph crushed the root into a white paste using an old-fashioned mortar and pestle.

'Remember what I called this?' he said, gesturing to the root.

'Was it shookum?'

'Skookum,' Randolph said. 'It means very, very strong.'

'It's just a root,' Jesse said.

Randolph took Jesse's hand and folded all the fingers down except one. Then he took that one finger and touched it to the paste. A second later, Jesse tasted something tart in his mouth. He'd never tasted anything like it before.

'Hey!' He gasped, backing away. 'I can taste it!'

Randolph just nodded. Jesse suddenly realized why he'd done that.

'That stuff's pretty strong,' he said.

Randolph started grinding the root again and adding the other ingredients.

'When we're done with this, it'll be even stronger,' he said. 'Our medicine is one that you have to be very sick to use. If you're not sick, it's so strong it will kill you.'

It wasn't long before Randolph was finished. Using the alder stick, he scraped the grainy whitish paste out of the pestle and into a hand-carved wooden bowl.

'I guess a beaker wouldn't do, huh?' Jesse said.

'That's right,' said Randolph. 'Now, come on.'

They went out again, climbed into the pick-up and drove down to the cove. There they made for the jetty.

'Shouldn't we be rowing a birch-bark canoe?' Jesse asked, only half kidding.

'It's in the shop,' Randolph replied, climbing down into the small rubber dinghy that Jesse had used the day before.

Jesse climbed in and they started to row out into the cove. It was evening now and the air was still; the surface of the water was like glass. As they got further away from the emergency centre, the only sound Jesse could hear was the dip and splash of the oars. It seemed as if the whole world had suddenly grown quiet, waiting for this solemn moment when the Haida medicine would be administered.

Now Jesse could hear another sound — the laboured wheezing and gurgling of a sick whale. Not far away, Luna floated. Jesse had just begun to wonder where Willy was when the whale suddenly surfaced, right next to the dinghy, and stared straight at Jesse as if asking what he planned to do now.

Jesse locked eyes with his friend, trying to tele-graph the importance of the moment. The other medicine hadn't worked. This was their last chance. Randolph nodded at Jesse. Jesse gave Willy the sign to open his mouth.

Willy opened his mouth. A few feet away, Luna did the same. Jesse picked up the wooden bowl and held it for Randolph, who scooped up the grainy white paste with a large leaf. Slowly, carefully, he began to apply the paste to Luna's tongue. Jesse almost winced at the thought of the taste, but he knew that these were very smart creatures. Somehow they understood that this was a good thing.

Randolph scooped more of the paste out of the bowl. He'd developed a rhythm to it. As if it wasn't only *what* he was giving to Luna, but also *how* he was giving it. The older man slowly closed his eyes and began to sing a soft song.

With one hand, Jesse reached out and stroked Willy to reassure him. Surely this song was part of the medicine. It was a healing song.

'It's going to be OK, Willy,' Jesse whispered. 'Luna's going to be OK. The medicine's going to work.'

Jesse kept stroking Willy, and Randolph kept singing. The song filled the silence until it seemed to Jesse as if there were others joining in; he could imagine a place in the woods, a Haida village where Randolph's tribesmen squatted near a fire, joining in the song, offering their spiritual support.

Jesse looked at Willy and saw a big drop of water at the corner of the orca's eye.

'Randolph?' Jesse asked in a whisper.

'Yes, Jesse?' Randolph replied, still humming the healing song.

'Can a whale cry?'

Randolph looked over at Willy. Of course Willy was in the water and was all wet, anyway. Maybe it was just Jesse's imagination.

'It's probably just seawater, Jesse,' Randolph said.

'Yeah.' Jesse nodded. 'You're probably right.'

But he only said that for Randolph's sake. Or maybe it was for Willy's sake. Because Jesse knew the whale and he knew what Willy was feeling. Jesse felt a pang deep in his heart. Willy was stuck here in this cove with his sick sister. And somewhere, out there in the straits, Catspaw was searching for them, calling for them, crying for them. And Jesse knew the feeling. He'd known it all his life. To be missing someone, to want them and not be able to get to them . . .

And then Jesse felt a tear slide down *his* cheek. And he knew Willy knew it wasn't seawater.

Behind him Randolph sang the healing song. By now Jesse was familiar enough with it to hum along. And then the most amazing thing happened: Willy began to whistle it. Jesse turned and gave Randolph a shocked look, but the older man only nodded knowingly. Now Littlespot rose in the water next to his big brother, and he began to sing, as if all their voices together would somehow add strength to the medicine.

And then, finally, another voice joined in, weak and faint. It was Luna.

It grew dark. Jesse and Randolph paddled slowly back towards the jetty. Far up on the beach, the emergency tent was aglow with lights and buzzing with activity, but here out on the dark water, it was still calm and quiet.

They reached the jetty and climbed up on to it. Jesse gazed back out into the dark, looking for Luna but unable now to see her. He felt Randolph's arm go round his shoulder.

'We've done everything in our power to help,' Randolph said. 'All we can do now is let them sleep.'

'Wait and see if the spirits are with us?' Jesse asked.

'The spirits are always with us,' Randolph said. 'But tonight we also need some luck.'

Randolph started to turn, but Jesse didn't.

'You coming?'

'In a little while,' Jesse said.

'OK.' Randolph set off along the jetty.

Jesse sat down at the jetty's edge. Willy surfaced close by. It was funny how Jesse knew that Willy would be there. Jesse bent down and spoke softly to him. 'I'll make a deal with you,' he said, thinking of the conversation he'd had with Nadine earlier that afternoon. 'You help Luna feel better. You lead your brother and sister out of this cove. You find your mother. You do that, and I'll do everything I can to keep your water clean and safe for as long as I live. OK?'

Willy blinked. Then he raised one of his flukes and waved it within Jesse's reach. Jesse took hold of the end of the fluke and shook it.

'Then it's a deal,' he said. 'I'm taking you at your word. And I'm holding you to it.'

18

The campsite was empty when Jesse got back to it that night. He knew that Annie and Glen were still out looking for Elvis. What a little jerk the guy was, running away at the very time when everyone should have been trying to help Willy and his brother and sister. But somehow Jesse also understood. He could see how *he* might have done the same thing when *he* was that age.

He roasted a hot dog over the fire, then washed his hands and crawled into his tent. It was funny but, even though he was all alone, he didn't feel lonely or scared. Maybe because he knew that so many people on the island felt the way he did. It was like they were all together in this effort to save those whales. He just hoped that, wherever Elvis was, he was OK.

Jesse was up at the crack of dawn. Elvis's sleeping-bag was empty. He couldn't imagine where the boy had spent the night. In the woods? In jail? Jesse quickly got dressed. He couldn't do anything about

Elvis right now, but he could go and see what was happening with Luna.

Outside, the tents were covered with dew. Jesse paused for a second outside Glen and Annie's tent. He could hear Glen snoring. So they'd come back without Elvis.

He hurried down through the woods to the emergency tent. Just as he got there, he noticed that Dr Haley was standing at the end of the jetty, looking out at the cove. Randolph was walking out towards her. Jesse quickly followed. As he got closer, he could see Willy circling, out in the cove, with Littlespot right behind him. And a third whale was splashing between them. Could it be?

Yes! It was Luna!

Dr Haley looked back at Randolph as he joined her on the jetty.

'How's it going?' he asked, but he had a smile on his face because he already knew.

Dr Haley was smiling. 'Looks like Luna's getting better.'

'My medicine is very powerful,' Randolph said, crossing his arms.

Dr Haley raised an eyebrow. '*Your* medicine?'

'Did I say that?' Randolph grinned. 'I mean, your medicine.'

Dr Haley smiled back. 'I don't know what you did, Randolph. But, whatever it was, I'm glad you did it.'

'So am I,' Jesse said, joining them.

Randolph put his arm round Jesse's shoulder. 'Let's just call it a group effort.'

They turned and headed back along the jetty towards the emergency tent.

'Is it time to get them back to Catspaw?' Jesse asked.

'Yes,' said Dr Haley. 'I just want to check on the currents. The last thing we want to do is lead them back into the oil spill.'

They went into the tent. Milner, the man from the oil company, was there again. He turned to a man Jesse had never seen before. This man was balding, with a ruddy complexion. He was heavy and his large belly protruded over the buckle of his belt.

'How's the containment going, Wilcox?' Milner asked.

'The slick will reach the cove pretty soon,' Wilcox replied. 'In a few hours I'm sealing off the cove with a boom to keep the oil slick out. We'll put out nets to keep the whales in. By that time, even if the whales could leave, they'd be swimming right into the slick.'

'Then I'm going out on the water now, to try and lead them to the open sea,' Dr Haley said.

This sounded to Jesse like the right thing to do, but he noticed Milner and Wilcox sharing an apprehensive glance. Then Milner took Dr Haley aside.

'Listen, Kate,' he said. 'I know you're going to be successful. I know you'll get them out of here before the oil comes. But, if you don't, we need a plan.'

Dr Haley eyed him suspiciously. 'And you have one in mind.'

Jesse was dying to hear what the plan was, but Milner led Dr Haley away and spoke to her in a whisper. Jesse watched their faces. Milner may have sounded earnest and honest but, deep down, Jesse didn't trust him. He could tell from Dr Haley's face that she didn't trust him completely either.

When they had finished talking, Dr Haley walked across to Jesse. 'Come on, you're coming with me.'

'What'd he say?' Jesse asked.

'It's not important,' Dr Haley replied. 'What's important is that we get those whales out of the cove before the oil gets here.'

They went out on to the jetty and got into the Zodiac. Jesse got into the front and they headed towards the whales.

When they got close to Willy, Jesse leant over the rail towards him.

'This is it, Willy,' he shouted. 'We've got to get you out of here now. You've got to make Luna leave. OK?'

Jesse looked back at Dr Haley and nodded. The Zodiac turned and headed towards the straits. Jesse scampered to the back of the boat and waved his arms.

'Come on, Willy! This way!'

Willy started to follow the boat, and Littlespot started to follow Willy. Luna brought up the rear, but she was moving slowly. Just as they got to the mouth of the cove, she dived, disappearing from sight. Jesse gave Dr Haley a worried look.

Luna came up again.

'Let's go, Luna!' Jesse shouted. 'How about a little sibling rivalry here? Your brothers are whipping your butt!'

Luna seemed to give a little more effort. Jesse looked around and saw that they were almost out of the cove now.

'Just a little further, and we're home free.' Dr Haley crossed her fingers.

Suddenly all three whales spouted and dived at once, disappearing beneath the waves. The driver of the Zodiac cut his engine. Jesse stared at the water for a sign of them, but he could see nothing.

'Where are they?' he asked.

'Maybe they're past us,' Dr Haley said. 'Underwater, heading out to the open sea.'

But Jesse had a bad feeling, and he looked back. His hope, that they had found freedom, was dashed. The whales had surfaced again — back in the cove.

19

The hope in Dr Haley's face vanished. The Zodiac slowed and turned around. Jesse stood in the bow and watched. Once again, Luna was floating listlessly in the middle of the cove. She must have been exhausted. The oil sickness must have weakened her more than they'd thought. Willy and Littlespot were swimming in restless circles round her.

Jesse caught Dr Haley's eye.

'We'll try again,' she said.

But Jesse shook his head. 'No. Luna's not ready.'

Dr Haley studied his face for a moment, then she nodded as if she knew he was right. They headed back towards the jetty. Nadine and Randolph were waiting there for them. John Milner and a group of other people passed them, making for the end of the jetty. Randolph was looking disappointed.

'Luna must not have the strength,' Jesse tried to explain.

'It's not just that,' Randolph said. 'They've given the order to boom off the cove, seal it completely to keep out the oil and protect the whales.'

Out in the cove, two large, white fishing boats were laying down the long yellow boom, while two smaller, grey boats were putting out a net attached to white floats.

'Protect them?' Nadine gave him a withering look. 'Don't you mean *trap* them? It's not just the boom. They're putting down nets, too.'

'The nets are for the whales' protection,' Dr. Haley explained. 'An hour from now, if they were allowed to swim under the boom and out of the cove, they'd be swimming right into a massive oil slick. They'd die.'

'But if they're trapped in the cove, they'll never get back to their pod,' Jesse argued. 'They'll never get back to their family.'

It was clear that Dr Haley already knew that. She nodded. 'You saw what happened when we tried to lead them out of the cove. They wouldn't leave. Luna's not ready. This is the best we can do.'

But anger and frustration were building in Jesse. The thought of Willy, Luna and Littlespot never seeing Catspaw again made him erupt.

'No, it's *not* the best you can do!' he yelled. 'Not hurting them in the first place would have been the best! Not ruining their home would have been the best! This is just a bunch of bull!'

'But Jesse —' Dr Haley started to say.

Jesse didn't hang around to listen to any more of

her stupid explanations. He'd had it with these adults and their stupid excuses. He stormed off along the jetty, not sure where he was going, but certain that he didn't want to stay and hear what they had to say.

As he passed the emergency tent, the sound of a television caught his attention. A group of emergency workers were crowding round a small portable TV. On the black-and-white screen was Milner, that man from the oil company. He was being interviewed in a studio somewhere. Since Milner was now out on the jetty, Jesse knew that the interview must have been taped earlier.

'We at Benbrook Oil are pleased to announce we have arranged for the whales to be lifted out of the cove this afternoon and taken to a marine rescue centre where they can be properly cared for while they recuperate,' he was saying.

Jesse felt a hand slide into his. He turned and found Nadine beside him, looking up at him.

'At least they'll be saved,' she said.

Jesse shook has head. 'It's no excuse for what happened.'

Suddenly the interview on the TV was cut off. A harassed-looking news reporter appeared in its place; he was pressing an earplug into his ear. He was evidently standing on a cliff overlooking a body of water. Behind him a fire was raging . . . A fire on *the water*!

'This is Ken Rogers with Channel Seven Eyewitness news,' the reporter said hastily. 'We're coming to you live from a bluff near Lawson Reef, the site of the *Dakar* oil spill disaster a few days ago. As you can see, behind me a new and devastating development has just taken place. According to our sources, a crew attempting to repair the ship a few hours ago accidentally ignited fuel vapours, causing an explosion. We've now learned that the oil slick itself is on fire. In a related development, all residents inhabiting the islands in and around Haro Strait are being asked to evacuate at this time.'

Jesse and Nadine stared at each other with wide eyes.

'Evacuate?' Jesse said, amazed.

'They'll have to get the whales out first,' Nadine said.

They both turned and looked back out at the cove. The white-hulled fishing boats were out there, trying to herd the whales together. One of the boats had a large hoist with a sling on the end of it to lift the whales out of the water. In the distance, over the straits they could see a cloud of dark grey smoke – from the burning oil.

Someone was tugging at Jesse's shirt. He turned around and found Elvis standing behind him.

'Where the heck have you been?' Jesse asked.

'Saving your blubbery butt,' Elvis replied.

Jesse made a face. 'What are you talking about?'

'I'll tell you, but you have to trust me,' Elvis said.

'Why should I trust *you*?' Jesse asked.

'Because nobody ever has,' Elvis said.

Jesse studied the boy's face. He was completely serious. For once he was telling the truth.

'Come with me,' Elvis said. He started to jog back on to the jetty. Jesse and Nadine followed. Elvis stopped about half-way out along the jetty.

'You see that guy?' Elvis pointed at Milner, who was standing on the end of the jetty and watching the rescue effort.

'Yeah, he's the guy from the oil company,' Jesse said.

'Right,' said Elvis. Then he pointed to one of the fishing boats in the cove. Wilcox, the heavy-set man, was standing on the deck of the boat, directing the people who were trying to save the whales. 'See that guy?'

'Yeah.'

'His name's Wilcox,' Elvis said.

'I know. So?'

'So about an hour ago I was sitting in a doughnut shop in Friday Harbour,' Elvis said. 'Like waiting for the next ferry to get me off this stupid island – and guess who sat down in a booth behind me?'

'I don't know,' Jesse said, getting a little annoyed. 'Ren and Stimpy?'

'No, those two guys,' Elvis said. 'Milner and Wilcox. And Wilcox starts talking about how he hasn't taken an orca out of the wild in twenty years.'

'That's right,' said Nadine. 'They're not allowed to any more.'

'Except Wilcox says he's got three right in his hands,' Elvis said.

Jesse and Nadine shot another look at each other. It was obvious which three whales Wilcox was talking about.

'Wilcox offered Milner a million dollars each for Luna and Littlespot, and two million dollars for Willy, because he's already trained,' Elvis said. 'He said the males are good because they can breed them, and he said Willy was a gold mine.'

It sounded like an outrageous lie, but Jesse had a feeling that Elvis was telling the truth. 'What did Milner say to all this?'

'He said Wilcox had to be careful to make it look like he had the whales' best interests at heart,' Elvis said. 'Then Wilcox said he did. He said the whales were really sick and they would need long-term rehabilitation.'

'Wait a minute,' Nadine said. 'This doesn't make any sense. First you tell us Wilcox offered Milner four million dollars for the whales. Then you tell us he's paying all that money just to rehabilitate them?'

'He wants to rehabilitate them,' Elvis said. 'But he also plans to charge people money to see them. He's gonna put them in the kind of place Willy used to be in. When he said long term, he meant *really* long term.'

Jesse gritted his teeth and made a fist. 'I knew it! I knew this was all too good to be true. The only reason they're saving those whales is to sell them into captivity. They'll never get back to their family.'

The next thing Jesse knew, he was running along the jetty as fast as his legs could carry him.

20

By the time Jesse reached the end of the jetty, the men on the boats had got Littlespot into the sling. The small whale was whistling and crying out in fear. Willy was floating near by, watching. Milner was standing with Randolph and Dr Haley. Jesse stormed up to him, with Elvis and Nadine right behind him.

'You're a liar!' he shouted. 'You're not trying to help these whales! You're selling them to an aquarium!'

'Jesse, stop.' Dr Haley stepped between them. 'I assure you that they'll be returned to their natural habitat as soon as they're ready.'

Elvis pointed at Wilcox, out on the fishing boat. 'Not if he has anything to do with it!'

'What are you talking about?' Randolph asked.

'You're going to lock 'em up and throw away the key!' Jesse yelled.

Dr Haley and Randolph both gave Milner a questioning look.

'I'm afraid you kids are going to have to leave,'

Milner said, nodding to some of his assistants.

Jesse could see they were going to get herded away. He darted round Dr Haley and came face to face with the man from the oil company.

'You promised you'd try to get them back to their mother!' Jesse shouted. 'You're not going to get away with this!' He gave Milner a push.

Splash! The man from the oil company fell off the jetty and into the water.

'Jesse!' Dr Haley gasped, stunned. But Jesse noticed a smile appear on Randolph's face.

'Get 'em, Willy!' Jesse shouted, signalling Willy towards the boat with Littlespot on it.

Willy instantly dived. Wilcox and the men in his boat rushed forward to the rails, searching the water for him.

Ker-Splash! The next thing Jesse knew, the boat rose into the air and flipped over, spilling the men into the water. Willy had tipped it over with his nose! Littlespot slid out of the sling and was free again! The men rose to the surface of the strait, spitting water and gasping for breath.

In the commotion that followed Jesse grabbed Elvis and whispered something to him. Elvis nodded and ran off. Meanwhile, Jesse and Nadine went down the jetty to the *Little Dipper*, Glen's boat.

Jesse jumped off the jetty and landed in the boat. He quickly started to untie the lines. Nadine stayed on the jetty.

'What are you doing?' she gasped.

'Hop in,' Jesse said.

'You know how to drive this thing by yourself?' Nadine asked uncertainly.

'Don't worry about it,' Jesse said. 'Just get in!'

Nadine didn't budge. 'Where did Elvis go?'

'He's going to take care of something for me,' Jesse said, flicking the ignition switch. 'You coming or not?'

Varrrroooomm! The engines roared into life and *Little Dipper* began to pull away from the jetty. At the very last second, Nadine hopped on board. Jesse steered towards the swimming platform just as a soaking wet Elvis was pulling himself out of the water. Jesse edged the boat up to the platform.

'All set?' he asked.

'Yeah.' Elvis hopped on board. 'Let's get out of here!'

Jesse gunned the engine and headed towards the boom that was blocking the entrance to the cove. Nadine and Elvis held on to the console.

'You know how to drive this thing?' Elvis yelled.

'Not really,' Jesse yelled back. As the boat neared the boom, Jesse pulled back on the throttle and let it idle. 'Willy!' he shouted.

Willy surfaced near the boat. Littlespot came up next to him and Luna trailed behind. On the jetty, some men were pulling Wilcox out of the water. He was shouting something about getting the kids.

Jesse reached over the side of the boat and rubbed Willy on the snout.

'We're getting out of here, OK,' Jesse said. 'Now pay attention. Here's one from the old days.'

He gave Willy the signal to jump. Willy nodded and chattered.

'You remember?' Jesse grinned. 'Great. They want you to be a captive whale. Let's give 'em a show!'

Willy dived beneath the surface. For a second everything was quiet.

'What did that signal mean?' Nadine asked.

'You'll see.' Jesse got behind the wheel of the *Little Dipper* again and raced the engine. This time he was steering straight for the boom.

'You can't crash into it!' Elvis yelled. 'We'll never get through!'

But Jesse held the throttle down, aiming for the centre of the boom. They were closing in on it fast. Forty yards, thirty . . . twenty . . .

'Jesse!' Nadine screamed.

Suddenly the water in front of the boat parted and a huge black-and-white torpedo burst into the air. It was Willy, filling the sky like a hot-air balloon.

'Holy mackerel!' Elvis shouted.

'Holy orca!' shouted Jesse.

Crash! Willy hit the boom with a tremendous splash. The boom collapsed, leaving a gaping hole. Jesse steered straight through it, then quickly turned and switched off the motor.

'What about Luna?' Nadine asked.

Jesse nodded back towards the cove. Willy and Littlespot were nudging their tired sister through the hole in the boom. Some of the people on the jetty were cheering and clapping, but Wilcox and some others were running towards another boat.

'They're coming after us!' Nadine cried.

'Guess again,' Elvis said with a devilish look.

Wilcox and his men jumped on board the boat and sped away from the jetty. Wilcox clambered to the prow of the boat and pointed at Jesse and the whales. Little did he know that Elvis had tied the anchor-line to the jetty.

Sproing! The anchor-line pulled tight, and the boat came to a sudden stop.

Ker-splash! Carried forward by their own momentum, Wilcox and his men crashed into the water!

'All right!' Elvis shouted.

'Look!' Nadine shouted, pointing ahead. Willy and his brother and sister were heading out into the strait, spouting and diving and calling.

Jesse turned the boat around and started to follow them. Suddenly he realized that the air above them was dark with thick, grey smoke. Looking ahead he saw why.

The strait was on fire!

21

'Where're the whales?' Jesse shouted to Elvis, who was in the bow.

'I don't see 'em!' Elvis shouted back. 'They must be under the water.'

The *Little Dipper* was in the drifting smoke now. Nadine looked scared.

'Jesse!' she yelled. 'We have to go back!'

'Not until I make sure they get past the oil,' Jesse replied.

Meanwhile the smoke was growing thicker. Jesse coughed. He looked around and realized that he couldn't see San Juan Island any more. He felt a hand placed on his forearm. It was Nadine's.

'Jesse,' she said, 'I'm scared.'

'Me, too,' Jesse said.

Up in the bow, Elvis leant over the side and dipped his hand in the water. When he brought it up, Jesse could see that it was black with oil.

'I think we're in trouble,' Elvis yelled, wiping his hand on his shirt.

'Any sign of the whales?' Jesse shouted back.

'I don't see anything except smoke,' Nadine said, and she coughed. 'Jesse, we have to turn around.'

'OK — just tell me which way is around,' Jesse said.

'Oh, no,' Nadine gasped. 'I can't tell!'

'Hey, you guys,' Elvis called to them from the bow.

'What?' Jesse asked.

'I see something in the water.'

'Whales?' Nadine asked hopefully.

'No, more like —'

Crunk! The *Little Dipper* suddenly shuddered, throwing everyone forward. The boat came to a stop.

'Rocks.' Elvis finished the sentence.

They could hear the sound of water rushing in somewhere below the waterline. The *Little Dipper* began to list to one side. Although Jesse had never spent much time on boats, he knew what that meant. They were sinking!

Elvis looked really scared. 'If you get me out of this, I'll swear to never touch your stuff or cross the line or say bad things about you ever again.'

'Promise?' Jesse asked.

Elvis nodded.

'I'm not going to let anything happen to you,' Jesse said.

Nadine coughed. Elvis coughed. The smoke was growing thicker and thicker.

'Hey, you feel something?' Elvis asked.

Jesse stood still. Oh, no, it was heat!

'The fire must be getting close!' Elvis shouted.

Thump-a-thump-a-thump-a ... Now they heard another but more distant sound gradually growing louder.

'A helicopter!' Jesse shouted.

'Hey! We're down here!' Everyone started to wave and shout up through the smoke. Meanwhile, the *Little Dipper* slid off the rocks and was beginning to roll with the waves. The water in the boat was knee deep.

From the helicopter above, a harness on a cable descended. Jesse reached up and grabbed it. They all locked eyes. Jesse then helped Elvis into the harness and as it started to rise, Jesse realized that he was sweating: it was the heat from the fire. He couldn't see it through the smoke, but it had to be close.

'You're the best brother I ever had!' Elvis called down to him from above as the harness rose.

'I'm the *only* brother you ever had,' Jesse yelled back.

The harness rose higher. Elvis looked white with fear.

'I'm scared!' he whimpered.

'Don't worry, kid!' Jesse shouted at him. 'It's just like bungee-jumping.'

'I never went bungee-jumping!' Elvis shouted back. 'I lied!'

You don't say, Jesse thought. A second later, the harness had disappeared into the smoke above. Meanwhile it was getting hotter. Jesse felt as if he was standing next to the campfire.

The harness came down again. Nadine didn't want to leave Jesse behind.

'Jesse —' she gasped.

'Go!' Jesse shouted back. 'There's only room for one!'

'You go!' Nadine said.

'No way!' Jesse shouted back. He grabbed her arm and helped her into the harness.

As she disappeared upwards, the boat sank further into the water. Jesse squinted up through the smoke. Where was the harness?

Suddenly he saw something — but it wasn't the harness. It was the flames! They were coming towards him, travelling across the oily water. Jesse had to shield his eyes with his hands. The heat and smoke were so great he couldn't stand them!

Where was that harness?

Suddenly, it dropped down through the smoke. Jesse grabbed it. His hands were covered in oil, but he thought he could climb into it. The flames were just a few feet away. It was so hot that he couldn't breathe!

'Go!' he screamed.

'Are you secure?' a voice from the helicopter shouted back.

He was covered all over in oil. The flames would be on him any second.

'I'm on!' Jesse screamed, holding on for dear life. 'Just go! *Go!*'

Suddenly he felt himself lift up from the boat. He was only about one-third into the harness and he kept trying to pull himself into it fully, but his oily hands were too slippery!

The harness was rising. If he could just hold on!

His hands were slipping!

Above him the smoke cleared. He could see the helicopter. He could see one of the crewmen reaching towards him. He could see Nadine's face, her eyes wide and frightened.

Jesse slid back. Now he was holding on just by his fingertips!

Only a few feet more to the helicopter.

'Hold on!' Elvis shouted.

Jesse tried to hold on for all he was worth.

'I'm slipping!' he yelled.

'Take my hand!' the crewman shouted.

Jesse reached for him and let go of the harness.

For a second he hung by one hand, holding on to the crewman's hand.

Then he slipped out of the man's grip, and he fell.

22

He was falling back into the smoke and flames.

WHAP! He hit the water so hard that it stunned him.

Then he was submerged. The water felt cool, even refreshing. He opened his eyes and looked up. It was like looking at clouds and sky. The dark clouds were the patches of burning oil. They had orange and crimson edges. The blue patches must be uncovered water, he thought.

He swam up and broke the surface in a blue patch. He gasped for breath. The air coming into his lungs was hot, like a steam bath.

'Help!' he gasped.

The flames were too hot; he could feel them scorching his face. He took another breath then dived down.

He was under the water again. How long could he last? Looking up from under the surface, it was mostly black clouds above him now. He couldn't see a spot with enough blue to go up to and get another breath! His lungs were starting to ache for air. He felt bubbles starting to dribble from his lips. Oh no! Oh No!

A shadowy form was moving towards him. At first Jesse didn't understand. Then he realized . . .

It was Willy!

The whale slowed down and passed by, very near him. His big whale eye looked at Jesse and blinked. Jesse grabbed his dorsal fin and Willy shot forward.

They came up in a blue patch, and Jesse gasped for air and held on to Willy's curled dorsal fin for dear life. But they were surrounded by flames. They couldn't stay here.

There was nowhere to go . . .

Except down.

'Go for it, Willy!' Jesse shouted. 'Go for it!'

He took a deep breath and pinched his nose with the fingers of one hand. He and Willy shot back down into the water, racing faster than Jesse had ever gone before underwater. He could barely hold on!

Where was Willy going?

What did it matter?

The sea was covered with flames . . .

Jesse felt his lungs start to ache again. He was going to have to let go.

Then a dark shadow appeared in the water ahead of them . . . a boat!

The water round it was blue!

Jesse let go. He struggled to the surface and took a delirious breath. He was so weak he could hardly stay afloat.

'Jesse!' Someone screamed.

Jesse twisted his head around. It was Annie! And Glen! And Randolph! Then the boat must be the *Natsalane*!

Hands reached down and held him under the arms. Jesse felt himself being lifted out of the water and pulled on board. He looked back down into the water and saw a familiar sight: Willy lolling near by.

'You saved his life, Willy,' Annie said.

It was true. Jesse grinned and felt the seawater drain out of his hair and run down his face. He waved at the killer whale. 'Thanks, Willy.'

23

They'd just wrapped Jesse in a blanket when the helicopter appeared and hovered over the deck of the *Natsalane*.

'We need to find some more people,' a crewman shouted down. 'Can you take these two?'

Nadine and Elvis stuck their heads out through the doorway behind the cockpit.

'Yeah, we'll take 'em!' Glen shouted back.

Nadine and Elvis climbed into the rescue harness and were lowered down to the deck. As soon as they had got out, the crewmen raised the harness and the helicopter swung away.

'I thought we'd lost you!' Nadine cried, and she threw her arms round Jesse. She hugged him as hard as she could.

Meanwhile Elvis was standing in front of Glen and Annie, looking sheepish. 'You don't have to say it. I know I shouldn't have run away. In fact, I ground myself.'

Annie knelt down and hugged him. 'And I'm sorry I broke my promise. It'll never happen again.'

Randolph had climbed up on to the bridge and was steering the boat away. 'Catspaw!' he shouted.

Jesse looked up quickly. 'Where!'

Randolph pointed ahead, out where the water was still blue and not covered by oil. Jesse and the others peered out and saw Catspaw and the other members of the pod. Jesse went to the side of the boat and leaned towards Willy.

'You did it, boy,' he said. 'You found her.'

Jesse expected that Willy would swim off, but the whale stayed beside the *Natsalane*.

'Go on,' Jesse urged him. 'You have to go. You'll be with your family again.'

Willy let out a soft, sad whistle. Jesse knew what he was saying. He could feel tears welling up in his eyes.

'I don't want you to go either,' he said. 'But you have to. You have the best thing anybody could ever ask for. You have your family. You have your mom.'

Willy let out a little cry. Glen came and stood beside Jesse.

'He won't leave,' Glen said.

'What's he waiting for?' Jesse asked.

Now Randolph joined them. 'He's waiting for you to give him the signal.'

He was right.

Jesse bit his lip. Once he sent Willy away, he might never see him again. But he had to do it! He *had* to! Jesse could feel the tears streaming down from his eyes as he pointed towards the pod ahead of them. 'I love you, Willy,' he gasped.

Then he gave the signal to go.

Willy's great eye blinked. He swam off to one side, dived, then leapt high in the air, spinning slowly and flapping his flukes at Jesse.

Splash! He hit the water and showered everyone on the boat. Seawater mixed with the tears on Jesse's face. He closed his eyes and felt Glen's arms go round him; Annie's arms went around him, too.

The *Natsalane* slowed. Jesse opened his eyes. The pod of whales had gathered together. They were spy-hopping, chattering happily, rubbing up against one another as if welcoming Willy and his brother and sister home.

24

Jesse and Nadine stood at the bow of the *Natsalane* as it headed back to the island. A fresh wind was in their faces. The sky ahead was clear blue. The smoke and fire were behind them.

Nadine squeezed Jesse's hand. 'You could come back next summer. When Willy's pod returns.'

Next summer? Jesse turned and looked at her. 'Can't we do something before that?'

Nadine smiled. 'You mean, without Willy?'

Jesse nodded and leant towards her. Hopefully no one else was watching.

At that moment Elvis appeared and stood before them.

'What are you looking at?' Jesse asked.

'What are *you* looking at?' Elvis shot back. Then he reached into his pocket and handed Jesse a creased and dog-eared photograph. Jesse looked down at it and felt his eyes widen. His whole body tingled and goose-pimples ran along his arms.

'It's for you,' Elvis said. 'It's why I hated your guts.'

Jesse stared down at the photo of himself and his mother. He was just a little kid, maybe four years old, when it was taken. Both he and his mother were grinning. They looked happy. For that moment, at least, they must have *been* happy.

The photo had been ripped in half, right down the middle, splitting Jesse from his mum. But then it had been taped back together.

'It's the only picture I ever had of her,' Elvis said. 'And *you* had to be in it. It kind of had an accident. But I taped it back together.'

Jesse looked at his half-brother. Now he knew for sure that under that wise-guy, know-it-all exterior was a good kid. A kid who'd been hurt just like he had, but a kid who was trying to deal with it and not let it get the better of him.

'Thanks, Elvis,' Jesse said. And he really meant it.

Elvis looked away towards the island, then back at Jesse. 'There's one more thing,' he said. 'Remember how I said she never talked about you?'

Jesse nodded.

'Well, she talked about you all the time,' Elvis said. 'She never stopped talking about you. She really missed you, Jesse. She really felt bad about what happened.'

The words made Jesse feel light-headed. He'd always wondered. He'd always *wished* . . . Now he knew. She'd cared. She'd felt bad about what had happened.

'She loved you,' Elvis said.

Jesse didn't even think about what he did next. He just reached out to the kid and hugged him.

Annie and Glen came on to the foredeck.

'So what do you think?' Annie asked her husband.

'I guess we can keep him,' Glen replied. 'I mean, I would hate to break up the set.'

Jesse let go of Elvis, and they both looked at Annie and Glen. Both of them had red-rimmed eyes.

'So what do you say, Elvis?' Glen asked. 'You want to stay with us? Be part of the family?'

Elvis pressed a finger against his lower lip. 'Uh, can I get back to you on that?'

'No,' Glen said. 'This offer expires immediately.'

'Hey, I was just kidding,' Elvis said. 'Just kidding. This has been the coolest vacation I've ever been on!'

Annie gave him a look. 'Oh, come on, Elvis, I bet you always say that.'

'No, honest, I'm telling the truth,' Elvis said. Then he looked a little sheepish and added, 'For once.'

They all laughed. Jesse put his arm round Nadine's shoulder and squeezed her. This was his family now. And it was the best he'd ever had.